Special Commission

By the same author

Special Commission

John Hall

**BREESE
BOOKS
LONDON**

First published in 1999 by
Breese Books Ltd
164 Kensington Park Road, London W11 2ER, England

ISBN: 0 947 533 93 1

Typeset in 11/14pt Nebraska by
Ann Buchan (Typesetters), Middlesex
Printed and bound in Great Britain by
Itchen Printers Ltd, Southampton

Kyme marched over, followed by Ralph and the others, and could now see that Bertram was crouching over a huddled figure that lay in the shadows.

'Well, man? What is it?'

Bertram looked up at Kyme, the tears streaming down his face, but could not bring himself to answer.

'This is ridiculous. Ralph, take a couple of these fellows and get him to his feet.'

Ralph and two of the servants bent over the figure on the ground. Bertram moved aside, and made no attempt to help them as, with something of an effort, they turned it over.

Ralph said, 'Come on, sir, up you get,' then he swore and stepped back hastily as he saw the knife, and the blood.

One

Spring had come early that year, 1449, and as the little procession, two riders out in front, a heavy cart, drawn by a pair of great, sturdy, farm horses, creaking along behind, and a child's pony carrying a tiny, hooded figure by the side of the cart, moved along the tiny street that formed the hamlet of Kyme, the dust blew up in great billows.

One of the two horsemen, a big man of perhaps fifty years, nodded towards the Maypole that stood on the little green before the great house. 'And shall I have the pleasure of seeing you prancing round that, good Bertram?'

'Many a long year since I did anything of that sort, Master Wood,' said Bertram, a tall thin fellow of thirty. He stared at the Maypole without any noticeable enthusiasm, then followed Wood towards the gate of Kyme.

The first house here had been built some three or four centuries ago, at the time of the Conqueror, a family house for the lord of the manor. Succeeding generations had added to the place, building on to it in a seemingly haphazard fashion, yet always keeping the basic original form, a single great hall for dining and – so far as the servants were concerned – sleeping. Even today the house had only a few private chambers, and those were reserved for the use of Lord Kyme and his family. Each addition had strengthened the fabric, so that now the house was a castle in all but name, and proof against all but a prolonged or a very determined siege.

At some point a moat had been dug to surround the whole of the enlarged house, and now, covered with a thick green blanket of weed, the moat looked as if it had been there since time itself began.

It smelled like it as well, or so Bertram thought. He waved a hand energetically in front of a nose that a casual observer might not have thought particularly sensitive. 'This warm weather doesn't do anything for the smell of the old moat, does it?'

'Best get inside,' said Wood, as the cart started to lumber up the village street towards them. 'Stagnant water is known to be a haunt of fevers.'

Bertram, who had learned great respect for Wood's medical skills over the years, did not need to be told twice, but set off over the heavy wooden bridge that spanned the moat in front of the gate, and was the only way into Kyme. The bridge was fixed, not a drawbridge, but being wood it could be burned in an emergency, thereby closing Kyme to the outside world. Even now, when things, here at any rate, were relatively peaceful, Bertram was conscious of the fact that he might be watched from the tiny windows cut high up in the great wall that towered over him, though when he glanced nervously up he could see nothing.

Over the bridge, and you reached the great gateway, its two huge oak gates propped open, for all were welcome at Kyme today. The gateway was wide enough to admit the cart which followed Bertram through it and down a short tunnel formed by the very fabric of the defending wall, into the courtyard.

On the two or three previous occasions when Bertram had visited Kyme, years ago now, the courtyard had been empty, or all upon, but today it seemed thronged to overflowing, though a more leisurely examination revealed that there were only a score or so of people there. However, they were all somewhat different from the usual run of scullions or farm labourers that the visitor might have expected to see in such a place. In one corner two men were playing fiddles, while a young lad gave an occasional but enthusiastic bang on a drum that was nearly as big as he was. In the opposite corner, a blind man played the flute.

As Wood and Bertram made for the stables, there were plenty of friendly greetings from such of the Kyme servants as happened to be in the courtyard. And it seemed that a good many of them had duties which permitted them to be out there just now.

'You'd think they'd all be busy inside,' said Bertram with that undisguised resentment that only comes from seeing someone else dodging their legitimate responsibilities in order to enjoy themselves.

'Remember that most of them will be stuck indoors waiting at table once the feast begins,' Wood told him, 'so this is the only chance they'll have to see the tumblers. They'll dance to a livelier tune once the hungry crowds turn up clamouring to be fed.'

The smell of the moat was not quite so pronounced in the courtyard, but it was hot in here, unseasonably hot, not the baking heat of full summer but close, with the stone walls seeming to contain the heat rather than keep the place cool, though the corners, which were deep in shadow, looked inviting.

Bertram nodded towards the house. 'Here's Ralph, come to welcome us.'

Ralph was a big man, as tall as Wood himself, though slightly stouter, with a florid face that looked as if he had plunged it into the well that stood in one corner of the yard. He stopped in front of Wood, nodded a greeting, and mopped his brow yet again with a kerchief that was already ringing wet. 'Welcome back to Kyme, Master Wood, and you, Bertram. Good to see you again after so long. Hot, you say? You should take a look in the kitchen, it's like the nether regions in there. As you can see, we have a good many – guests – here at Kyme just now,' and he waved round the courtyard with a humourless smile, 'but there will be plenty of room for you. Fit in where you will, you know your way around well enough.'

'Is my lord at home?' asked Wood. 'I have some choice items for his consideration, should he chance to have a few moments to spare me to take a look at them.'

'I'm sure he'll be pleased to see you, as always,' said Ralph. 'His guests will arrive towards noon, as usual, so if you make your way to the great hall then, you'll be sure to see his lordship there.' He nodded at Bertram by way of farewell, and set off about his duties.

'H'mm,' said Bertram, making his way to a patch of shadow, 'I have known the day when Master Butler gave us a more hearty welcome. Perhaps a touch stand-offish, would you not say? Something on his dignity, our good Ralph? Almost as if he were a bit too good for the likes of us, think you?'

'Too many strangers at Kyme already today. What are two more new faces among all these?' and Wood waved a hand at the throng all around them. 'Besides,' he went on, lowering his voice, 'as my lord's star rises ever higher, so good Ralph feels himself ever further above ordinary mortals like us. A common fault, my Bertram, and one you ought to guard against.'

'I shall keep it always in mind, master. Though, truth to tell, I think I'm in little enough danger of a swollen head, if it's my master's reflected glory that shall cause it. Tell me,' he added hastily, before Wood could work this out, 'does Lord Kyme's star shine ever more brightly these days? I had not heard anything of the sort. But then, I have not the latest gossip from the court.'

'Kyme is Suffolk's man. Or rather he's his own man, but happy to let Suffolk speak for him.' Wood paused, as if wondering whether it were entirely wise to continue, then he added in a lower tone, 'Though indeed, if rumour be true, even Suffolk himself is none too safe these days. And only the neat change of subject there saved your skin.'

Bertram smiled and nodded absently, thinking about Suffolk. The Earl of Suffolk – or Duke as he was now, having been elevated earlier that very same year, Bertram corrected himself – had to all intents and purposes ruled England this past five years, the King being but a poor creature. Any man who would obtain favours from the King had to go through Suffolk. If indeed the process involved the King at all these days, for there were those who said that Suffolk no longer even bothered to ask for royal approval of what was already done.

Bertram did not really follow Wood's last remark, though, for the doings of men like Suffolk were incomprehensible to men like Bertram. After all, how on earth could a man who did as he pleased, without even asking for the King's approval, possibly be in any sort of danger? Before he could ask for an explanation, Wood's voice interrupted his reflections. 'Best look to our goods.'

Bertram looked towards the carters, who had climbed down from their seat and were now looking with a marked lack of enthusiasm at the heavy packages they would shortly be expected to unload. 'I'll have them put in the stables, along with the horses, they'll be better off out of the heat,' he said. He walked over to the carters, and gave them their orders.

Wood stood for a while, then walked over to the tiny figure still seated motionless on the pony. 'Now, my lady,' he said, 'we can hardly leave you in the stable, can we? I think perhaps the best thing we could do is to find my lady's maid, and find some temporary quarters for you.' He reached up and swung her down on to the ground, then held out a hand. She hesitated for a moment, then reached up and put her tiny hand in his great paw.

When a visitor to Kyme stood in the courtyard and looked about him, as Wood was looking about him now, he saw that the old part of the house formed one side of a squat rectangle. Traces of the original wooden building could be seen in the wall that looked on to the courtyard, massive beams peeping out here and there from the later stonework.

That old part, the original manor house which was now the great hall, was still the real heart of Kyme, where the eating and drinking took place, and the sleeping and love-making too, as far as most of the servants were concerned. Lord Kyme and his wife had a private chamber, as did one or two privileged servants, Ralph, and my lady's maid, but the rest of the servants slept in the straw on the floor of the great hall, just as their parents and grand-parents had done before them.

To left and right were the newer wings, holding stables, bake-house and brew-house. It looked as if the last two were busy making all ready for the feasting that there would be later that day, and Wood could not help smacking his lips like any uncouth churl.

The fourth side of the courtyard was the massive wall with the great gate through which Wood had just come. The wall was thick enough to hold small rooms, which were used for storage, or to kennel the dogs.

There was no entrance into Kyme save through the main gate in the wall, and then no entrance into the great hall except from the courtyard. There was a main door into the great hall, a huge thing of oak like those in the outer gate, and today that door stood propped open, to let some air into the place. There were other doors into the house from the courtyard, leading to the kitchens and other domestic quarters, and the great hall could be reached from these as well, by inside doors and passages. But in any event you must still cross the moat first and come through the gate, and unwelcome visitors were thus very effectively excluded.

It was to the huge main door of the great hall that Wood now went, leading the tiny figure by the hand. He paused a moment just inside the door, to let his eyes adjust to the darkness after the brightness of the courtyard. Then he went right in, and took a look round. The room was enormous, one of the biggest rooms that Wood had ever seen, and he was a well-travelled man. It was busy, too, the servants coming and going with dishes and flagons, getting the long tables ready for the meal that would begin in a few hours.

Wood stopped one of the servants, and began to speak to him, but the man gave an impatient little click of the tongue, then held up a hand and said, 'Your pardon, sir, but you'd best talk to Master Butler. We're a bit busy in here just now, as you may see for yourself,' and he nodded towards a dark corner, before hurrying off about his duties.

Wood looked where the man had pointed, and could just make out Ralph, standing by a door and watching the activity in the great hall. Wood started towards the corner, and Ralph held up a hand in greeting as he approached.

'Much to do, I see,' said Wood.

Ralph nodded. 'And I don't like to move too far from the buttery. It's all very well for my lord to ask all these rogues into the place, but who can say what they may not get up to?'

'Oh, I suspect they'll all be far too much in awe of my lord – and of you – to get up to any mischief. I doubt if they would dare as much as enter the house without being asked to do so. They'd be as much out of place in here as a virgin at Barnet Fair.'

'H'mm.' Ralph did not sound entirely convinced. 'You may be right. Still, it's my job to look after things in the house, just as Harry's is to look after things outside, and I intend to do that job properly.'

'I'll not disturb you, then. But I wanted to see my lady's maid, if she happens to be anywhere handy.'

'Janet? She'll be in her room, I should think, in the other part of the house. Stay here if it please you, Master Wood, and make sure that none of these vagabonds get into my pantry, and I'll fetch her, if she's not too busy.'

'My thanks, Master Butler.' Wood took up his post by the door of the buttery as Ralph went into the wing that held the private chambers. He glanced down at the tiny figure which still clasped his hand. 'What think you to Kyme, then, my lady?'

14

There was no reply.

'A bustling sort of place,' Wood went on, 'busy at all times, for it's a big old place, and takes a deal of work to keep it up, but all the more so today, for Lord Kyme likes to make a brave show on the feast days, the old feast days, Christmas and May Day. It's an old tradition at Kyme, a family tradition. Most of the gentlemen from round about will be here, and all the labourers and villagers from Lord Kyme's estates. Yes, it's a busy day.'

He gazed down at the tiny figure, as if hoping for some reply, but none came, and Wood seemed relieved when Ralph came back, accompanied by an elderly woman with a kind face.

Wood greeted the elderly lady with elaborate politeness, and told her, 'Janet, there's something you could do for me, if you would be so kind. My lady would approve, I know, and you'll do so too, once I've explained it to you,' and he went towards the door, Janet following.

Ralph could see Wood and Janet deep in conversation, the talk seeming to refer to the small figure that still held Wood's hand, for they looked down at her frequently. After a time, Janet held her hand out, and the small figure let go of Wood's hand, and took hold of Janet's, then allowed herself to be led out into the courtyard.

Wood stayed by the main door for a while, looking out after Janet, then he too left the great hall, and went across to the stables, where he sought out Bertram, and the two of them talked on a wide variety of subjects, all interesting enough to the two of them, but of no particular consequence otherwise.

The meal would start somewhat later than was usual at Kyme, to mark the fact that it was a special day. Lord

Kyme's neighbours would begin to arrive around noon, there would be merry-making round the Maypole on the village green for a couple of hours, and then the meal would be served around four o'clock.

When the sun was almost directly over the Maypole, the first of Lord Kyme's guests began to arrive. 'About time to make our own way inside, I think,' said Wood, with an inclination of the head towards the latest young gallant to ride into the courtyard. 'Once the polite greetings are out of the way, we shall see if my lord is eager to welcome our humble selves.'

'My lady certainly should be,' said Bertram, with a sidelong glance at his master.

Wood flushed a dull brick-red.

'I mean, because of the present we have for her,' added Bertram hastily. He knew that Wood disliked jokes about my lady, though they were harmless enough, God knew.

Wood stared at Bertram for a long moment, then his brow cleared, and he laughed aloud. 'Much may be forgiven on a feast day,' said he, 'but for all that, it's a wise man who knows when to keep his mouth shut. I doubt if my lord would be quite as tolerant as I am on that particular matter.'

Too true, thought Bertram. Not, of course, that he – Bertram – would ever have dared make any remark on the subject within earshot of Lord Kyme, much less Lady Kyme. Indeed –

'Well?' demanded Wood. 'Are you coming inside, or just standing there picking your nose?'

Bertram followed Wood inside the house. At one end of the hall, a small group of men, Lord Kyme's personal guests, stood talking together. Wood, being merely a merchant, albeit a wealthy one, did not have the same status as these men, who all possessed country estates. This was something that Bertram had often remarked upon in an uncomplimentary fashion, always ending up by saying sourly that Wood should invest some of his profits in land, so that he would be accepted as a gentleman, and Bertram himself would not be too far behind.

After a few moments, the murmur of conversation ceased, and Wood and Bertram looked towards the door, where a stout, bearded man of fifty or so had just come in, followed by a tall, attractive woman some twenty years younger.

Wood moved forward as this man, Lord Kyme, and his wife, came into the main body of the hall. Ralph, who must have gone through the buttery and courtyard, for they had not noticed him go through the hall, moved in a stately fashion behind his master and mistress. Behind Ralph there came a dwarf, clad, despite the heat, in a heavy black cloak trimmed with fur. The dwarf bowed gravely to the folk to his right and left as he walked along.

'Fortunato looks well,' said Wood in an undertone, nodding towards the dwarf.

'Aye. And he'll look even better when he sees what we've brought for him.'

Lord and Lady Kyme had reached the little knot of men, and paused to exchange a few words with them. Although the May celebrations and feasting were the ostensible reason for these guests being there, some of them took this opportunity to talk to Lord Kyme on more serious topics. Kyme was, after all, a powerful man, an associate of Suffolk, and had influence at court.

Wood had managed to edge his way towards the front

of the little crowd that surrounded Lord Kyme, so that when Kyme had greeted the last of his guests his eye lit on Wood. 'Ah, Master Wood, good to see you at Kyme once again. Do you have anything that might interest me today?'

'I flatter myself that I may have one or two items that may amuse your lordship.' Wood nodded to Bertram, who went out into the courtyard, to return a very short while later followed by the two carters, who carried between them a wooden cage, in which sat a small but vicious-looking monkey.

Kyme clapped his hands when he saw this. 'Wonderful,' he said. Then he added, not in any unkindly fashion, 'A friend for you, Fortunato.'

Fortunato bowed deeply. 'I thank your lordship. It is true I have been somewhat short of intelligent company this past ten years. In two days, I'll have this little fellow talking as well as I do myself. Nay, more, within the week I'll have him capering as lively as does your lordship.' And he had to jump out of the way as Kyme aimed a playful blow at his head.

Wood laughed with the rest, then said, 'I fancy your lordship will find that we can do far better than that for good Master Fortunato. But first, I have something else which I know your lordship will enjoy,' and he nodded a second time to Bertram, who led the carters outside in a stately procession, to return soon after with another cage, this one holding a large creature with something of the look of a great domestic cat about it, a creature which spat at the onlookers and clawed at the bars of its cage, causing those nearby to jump back and cross themselves hastily.

'Lynx?' asked Lord Kyme, eyeing the creature as warily as any of his guests.

'A civet, my lord. A fine thing to keep down the rats and mice that abound in an old house like this,' and he bowed to Lady Kyme.

'Indeed,' she said, eyeing the cage. And then, to her husband, 'I trust you won't be letting this creature roam about the place unchecked. I don't know about rats and mice, but I wouldn't answer for my own safety, let alone that of the kitchen cat.' Looking at Wood again, she went on, 'But you are, as always, most welcome at Kyme, Master Wood,' and she held out her hand, which Wood took hold of and kissed, for all the world like some courtier.

Was it his imagination, thought Bertram, or did my lord colour slightly at this gallantry? And to be sure, there was no good reason why he should not do so, for you scarcely expected a fine lady to hold out her hand to be kissed by a tradesman, even a fine man like Master Wood. There was something odd here, something you could not put your finger on. Perhaps, though, Bertram asked himself, Wood had indeed put his finger on it, as a man might say?

Bertram caught Lord Kyme's eye, and, with an effort, suppressed the laugh that had come unbidden to his lips. Did Kyme possibly wonder the same thing, but without being able to laugh about it, wondered Bertram? Certainly his stern face gave nothing away.

Kyme stared, fascinated, at the cage. 'I'll keep it safely locked away, so that old Tib's safe enough, not that she couldn't give a good account of herself, even against this. But yes, Master Wood, you're quite right, I must have this, whatever the cost. It will be the jewel of my collection. The start of a new collection, in truth, for the old one has failed to thrive, I fear. But am I mistaken, or did

I hear you say something about a present for Fortunato?'

'You did, my lord.' Wood waved a hand at Bertram, who stood by the door. Bertram went out briefly into the courtyard, returning almost immediately, his arm stretched out and down, his hand firmly held by a female dwarf, a womanly counterpart of Fortunato. There was an audible gasp from one of the labourers who had ventured inside the hall, for she was very attractive, and dressed in a style fashionable in London, though it is doubtful if anyone there, apart from Lady Kyme, was aware of that fact.

'Oh, how sweet,' said Lady Kyme. She hurried over to the tiny woman, little more than a girl, as Lady Kyme now saw, and held out her hands. 'What might your name be, my dear?'

'Isabella, my lady.' The voice was deep and confident, though the eyes looked anxious.

'Wonderful. I shall call you Bella, and you shall live here with dear little Fortunato, and be very happy.'

'Wedding bells, perhaps, eh, Fortunato?' asked Lord Kyme, a broad grin on his face.

The dwarf bowed to Kyme, then to Bella, a deep bow, that one, and finally to Wood.

Wood said, 'As soon as I set eyes on the girl, I thought of Fortunato.'

'You are too kind, Master Wood,' said Fortunato.

'And now,' said Kyme, 'business being done – and pleasure too, Fortunato – I think it's time to start our celebrations,' and he held out his arm formally to his wife, and, when she had taken it, led the way outside.

Fortunato held his arm to Bella, who looked at it for what seemed a long time, then, entering into the spirit of the day, she curtsied, took the offered arm, and went out after Lord and Lady Kyme, to the accompaniment of some ribald but good-natured remarks from those who stood round about.

Bertram nudged Wood in the ribs. 'Fortunato seems well pleased, eh, master?'

'I should think he does. Where would he find another such as Bella? And my lord seems equally well satisfied with his new pets. Which had best go back in the stable for now, I think.'

'And the payment, master? The payment?'

'Oh, I shan't press for that. My lord, or Ralph more like, will attend to that before we leave in the morning. Let's not worry about that just for now.'

The labourers from the Kyme fields and woods had all arrived by now, and for the most part they stood around the village green in silence, embarrassed at being there, or so it seemed, until Lord Kyme had made a short speech of welcome, and the musicians came out in procession and began to play, after which the day became more of a holiday.

The custom at Kyme was to have a short celebration, no more than two or three hours by the clock, outside, then for the eating and drinking to take place in a slightly more formal manner in the great hall. Lord Kyme was firmly of the opinion that this feast, which all who lived and worked on the Kyme lands were expected to attend, made his labourers feel that they were truly part of the Kyme estates, instead of being welcomed only as far as the main gate, though an impartial spectator might have wondered, looking at their expressions as they began to trail into the courtyard, if the labourers fully appreciated this fact.

When Ralph emerged from the main door and told

him that all was ready, Lord Kyme spoke to one or two of the older villagers, who then saw to it that everyone made their way inside.

Large though the great hall was, it was crowded by the time that the latecomers got to their places. Bertram had half hoped that one of those girls who had been dancing round the Maypole might take a seat next to him, but he was disappointed, for the women and children sat together, close to the door.

They had just got decently into their stride with the great joint of beef which Ralph himself had set before them, when Bertram nudged Wood in the ribs and pointed to the high table. 'My lord looks somewhat upset.'

Lord Kyme looked more than upset, he looked downright angry. Ralph, who stood by his master's shoulder, had evidently not brought any good tidings, for Kyme's face turned a deep crimson and he slammed his hand down on the table in front of him. The music from the minstrels in the gallery faded away at the sound, so that Kyme's words, spoken in an angry roar, were audible throughout the hall. 'Get rid of him,' he told Ralph. 'I won't have him here at Kyme. I won't –' and he broke off as his wife laid a hand on his arm and said something in his ear. Kyme started to speak, but his wife did not let him, but carried on talking in a low, calm tone until he subsided, and gave a short laugh.

Lady Kyme let go of his arm. Kyme said something to Ralph, in a low voice, and the butler bowed and went out. The minstrels – actually the fiddlers and so on who had been playing on the village green earlier, and who had been induced to take on this new role – began playing again, the tumblers and jugglers began to move, and things were once more cheerful.

'I wonder what all that was about,' said Bertram, helping himself to ale.

Wood shrugged his shoulders. 'I shouldn't think my lord will see fit to confide in you and me. However, my lady seems to have sorted matters out in a satisfactory fashion, whatever kind of tangle they may have been in. Don't finish that off, man, I could do with another drink myself.'

Bertram frowned, and looked round for another jug of ale. When the food and drink had all but gone, many of the farm labourers began to leave, evidently not being really happy to be in the house without the excuse of the feast.

Wood, pleasantly relaxed by the food and drink, was startled by a tap on his shoulder, and he looked round, to see Fortunato standing there grinning at him. The dwarf bowed deeply, and Wood inclined his head in reply.

'Thank you once again for my present, Master Wood,' said Fortunato, perching on the edge of the table, and helping himself from Wood's mug of ale without waiting to be asked.

'Think nothing of it. Or, rather, thank Lord Kyme, for he'll be paying the reckoning. And how are things at Kyme these days? I must say, you look well. Does he not, Bertram?'

Bertram, who was busy drinking, took the mug from his mouth long enough to nod agreement. Fortunato gave him a bow as well, and said, 'I do tolerably well, you know. Save, perhaps, only in the one respect. A trifle to some, I know, but important when lacking.'

'What might that be?' asked Bertram, intrigued.

'Why, that very thing that good Master Wood has just provided for me in the shape of the lovely Bella.'

Wood laughed. 'You surprise me. I noticed more than

one very attractive kitchen maid, as I walked round earlier. Do you honestly tell me that you've had no success at all in that direction?'

'I tickle their sense of humour, it's true, but very little else. Now, a rich and handsome man like you, Master Wood, you could do great things. There, for instance,' and he pointed to the door of the buttery, from which a particularly attractive girl had just emerged.

'Who is she?' asked Bertram, sufficiently impressed to lower his mug of ale for a better look.

'One of those same kitchen maids.'

'I knew I should have become a cook,' complained Bertram.

Fortunato grinned happily at him. 'Don't tell me that there isn't a wench – if not two or three of them – that'll miss you tonight?'

'It's difficult to make the right sort of impression when you're as badly paid as I am.'

'Ah, there at least I score over you,' said Fortunato. 'I have all the fair lands of Kyme at my disposal, to say nothing of this great house. The only slight drawback is that giant jester of mine, who persists in the delusion that it all belongs to him.'

Bertram grinned at him. 'You get on well with Lord Kyme?'

'As well as a jester may get on with a lord, yes. It isn't too bad a life, provided that you have no strong objection to looking ridiculous now and then. And let's be honest, most men do that from time to time, if not all the time, without getting paid for it. Besides,' and Fortunato looked serious at this point, 'what else could I do?'

'You must have been here, what, ten years now?' asked Bertram.

'Nearer fourteen, you know. I was nine or ten, I believe, when first I came here.'

Bertram sighed, and made the usual response about the inexorable passage of time.

'Aye,' said Fortunato, 'on winged feet, indeed. Tell me, though, this Bella of yours, or ours, now, whence comes she?'

'Bella? Oh, Master Wood found her about a couple of months ago. A merchant – we've done a good bit of business with him over the years – came by with some goods.'

'And Bella was among them?'

'Aye. Master Wood thought of Lord Kyme – and you – at once.'

Fortunato gave Wood a stinging slap on the back. 'For which, my thanks again, Master Wood. Now, my lord will be missing my witty jests and inspired advice. A jester who fails to jest when there's a feast going on will not stay in favour quite as long as he might wish.' He jumped down from the table, gave them a last bow, and made off towards the other side of the room.

Wood stood up as well. 'Too much ale,' he said, with a wry grin at Bertram. 'I'll be back shortly,' and he set off for the door.

Bertram, thus deserted, looked round the hall and became aware for the first time of how few people were left in there. He remarked on this fact to one of those who remained, a short, squat man with a surly expression, who was now Bertram's closest neighbour though he sat six feet from him, the intervening seats having been vacated.

This man initially did no more than shrug at Bertram's remark, but mature reflection seemed to encourage him somewhat, and he moved closer, to launch into a long and detailed – a very long, and unnecessarily detailed, or so it seemed to Bertram – explanation, covering the state of the fields, the unseasonable drought, the harshness of the farm labourer's existence, and the unfairness of life in general. On he went, and on, and on, until at last he stopped, from sheer exhaustion as it seemed to Bertram.

'Well,' said Bertram, at last, 'it's been most amusing, and instructive, talking to you, but all this excellent ale is having its natural effect on me as well. Would there be a privy to hand, think you?'

'Privy? I dare say there's a dozen of them in a fine place like this. They'll all be for the fine ladies and gentlemen, though. You and me, we slash in the courtyard.'

'I suppose we do, at that. Excuse me, would you? Back in a moment,' and Bertram made his way to the door.

He had not been gone more than five minutes, when the relative peace of the hall was shattered by some disturbance near the main door. The remaining diners looked round with some curiosity, to see a young woman standing in the doorway, crying noisily, with occasional bursts of unintelligible speech. A group of men formed round her, asking what was wrong.

Lord Kyme, his conversation with his guests interrupted by this, looked up and asked angrily, 'What is it? What's the matter there?'

Ralph, who was in the group round the door, came forward and said, 'It's Daisy, my lord, one of the maids. Something has evidently frightened her, I think she's saying, "He's dead," but she won't say who, or anything which makes sense.'

Kyme stood up, and looked at his guests. 'Well, gentlemen, shall we see what this is all about?' He led the way to the little knot of men by the door, and they moved aside to let him through to the girl.

'Now, Daisy, is it? What is all this about?'

Daisy, overawed by this sudden attention from a man who up to then had not seemed aware of her existence, could not manage to speak at all, but merely waved a hand towards the door.

Kyme gave an angry snort, and said, 'It must be in the courtyard, whatever it is,' and strode outside. He stopped outside the door, and glared about him. 'Nothing out here. Ralph, take a look round, would you?'

Ralph made his way across to the stables, stopped abruptly, turned and waved an arm.

'Gentlemen?' Kyme led the apprehensive little group across the yard.

'Over there, my lord,' and Ralph pointed to a corner by the stables, where Bertram could just be seen, apparently seated on the ground.

Kyme marched over, followed by Ralph and the others, and could now see that Bertram was crouching over a huddled figure that lay in the shadows.

'Well, man? What is it?'

Bertram looked up at Kyme, the tears streaming down his face, but could not bring himself to answer.

'This is ridiculous. Ralph, take a couple of these fellows and get him to his feet.'

Ralph and two of the servants bent over the figure on the ground. Bertram moved aside, and made no attempt to help them as, with something of an effort, they turned it over.

Ralph said, 'Come on, sir, up you get,' then he swore and stepped back hastily as he saw the knife, and the blood.

Two

Amongst the other improvements over the years, a little dungeon had been built at Kyme. Nothing elaborate, just a little room built into the thickness of the outer wall, near the main gate, low down in the wall, so that the tiny slit which was all the place possessed by way of a window was almost on the same level as the surface of the moat. This meant that the walls of the dungeon were permanently wet and slimy to the touch, and the air had a dampness to it which reeked of the stagnant moat itself.

It was now April in the year 1450, and spring that year was unseasonably late, just as it had been early the previous year. A chilly breeze blew through the slit in the dungeon wall, bringing even more damp air from the evil-smelling moat into the little room, and causing the man who occupied the dungeon at the moment to curse vigorously, then mutter a prayer asking forgiveness for his lapse.

He had been in the dungeon for an hour or two now, and he felt that it was quite long enough. A clatter of horses' hooves on the wooden bridge, almost overhead, as it seemed to him, made him bend to look through the slit in the wall, but it was set at an angle in the thick stones, and he could see nothing. He could hear well enough to make out that it was a small party, though, ten or a dozen horses, and that, he knew, must mean that Clement had brought Sir George and the others to his rescue. He sighed. True, he would at least be freed from this damp cellar, but then he would have to face Sir George and his heavy irony. He sighed again.

After ten minutes' silence, he heard the heavy wooden bar which secured the door on the outside being lifted. His eyes had grown used to the darkness of the dungeon by now, and he blinked as the daylight came flooding in.

Two soldiers in livery helped him out of the dungeon and up the short flight of steps that led to the courtyard. 'Up you come, sir,' one of the soldiers told him. 'Sorry for the mistake. It's all sorted out now. And we'll soon have that little bit of muck off your tunic.'

The man who had been in the dungeon stood upright, stretching his back gratefully. He was a young man, twenty-five at the most, with good looks that were marred for the moment by an angry set of the jaw. As one of the men-at-arms made an ineffectual dab at the mould that he had acquired from the dungeon wall, he said, 'Leave it!' then added in a gentler tone, 'It'll brush off easily enough once it's dried.'

The man who had spoken to him said, 'That's the spirit, sir. No harm's done, and we're all very sorry for the mistake, I'm sure, sir. And his lordship will tell you the very same thing, I know, when he sees you. The other gentlemen are with him now, and they're all waiting to see you.'

'I'm sure they are,' said the young man wryly. He gestured at the livery the men wore. 'This is Kyme, I take it?'

'It is that, sir. I'm Harry, constable to his lordship.'

'I'm delighted to meet you, Harry. I'm Martin Byrd,

secretary to their honours, the Justices of the special commission.'

'So I understand, sir. Now.' Harry's face showed that the process of enlightenment had not been a pleasant one, and, knowing Sir George, Martin could sympathize with him. 'Glad to meet you, sir,' Harry went on, 'though I could wish it had been under better circumstances. But we'd best go, if you're quite ready, for I think the other gentlemen are impatient to see you.'

As he led the way across the courtyard, Harry asked, 'You'll be a clergyman, I take it, sir? With being able to read and write, I mean?'

'Yes, I've taken Holy Orders, though I decided on this work rather than do any pastoral duties.'

'It was the hair, you see, sir.'

Martin looked at him blankly.

'With you not having the – what's it called, now?'

'Oh, the tonsure, you mean. No, not all of us who have been taught by the Church bother with that, not these days.'

'No, and that's why we thought you were – well, you know. But you can still do the forgiving, and all the rest of it?'

'Why, I trust I can, as much as any Christian, so you need not worry too much about our little misunderstanding this morning. Oh, but do you mean in the sense of formal absolution, perhaps?'

Harry nodded. 'Aye, that's it. Absolution, that was the word I was groping for.'

'Yes, I am able to do that, strictly speaking, although in actual practice I've never actually been asked to do it thus far.' Martin studied his guide closely. 'Of course, if there's anything you might need to confess, then your own parish priest is the man to speak to. I thought I saw a church not too far away from the main gate. Though I did have other things on my mind, I admit.'

'No, no, there's nothing like that.' Harry's sunburned face flushed. 'Well, nothing special, at any rate. No, I just wondered, that was all. Ah,' he went on, relief apparent in his voice, 'here we are.' He made as if to lead the way inside, but was halted by a large man with a dignified bearing and a florid face.

'Thank you, Master Constable,' said the man who blocked the doorway, 'I shall take over, if you please.'

'As you will, Ralph. See you again, perhaps, sir, on some happier occasion, we hope.'

'Master Byrd? I am Ralph, my lord's butler. This way, if you will,' and Ralph led Martin into the great hall, where a little group of men stood or sat at one end of a long table.

Ralph cleared his throat and announced, 'Master Byrd, my lord.'

'Thank you, Ralph.' The speaker was another tall man, seated at the table's head. He was bearded, and had an air of being obeyed that went with his expensive clothes, so that Martin would have recognized him as the owner of Kyme even without Ralph's words. 'Master Byrd, welcome to Kyme. You know these gentlemen, naturally,' and he waved a hand round the table.

Martin bowed to the three men who sat with Kyme, the special commissioners to whom he acted as secretary.

The head of the commission, Sir George Maryon, a burly man with close-cropped hair and a red face, who invariably reminded Martin of an innkeeper back in his home village – the similarity was increased at the moment by the ancient leather travelling coat Sir George still wore – looked up, snorted audibly, and said in his most provocative fashion, 'Decided to join us, then, Martin?'

Before Martin could speak, Kyme cleared his throat noisily, and said, 'Entirely the fault of my constable and his men, Sir George. They evidently mistook good Master Byrd here for a vagrant, and acted in a manner more zealous than inquiring. We are all a little on edge in these parts of late, I fear, following that dreadful business of Master Wood's death, even though it is a year or so since it happened. Nothing of that sort's happened at Kyme, in my lifetime at any rate, and it's made us unsettled. Suspicious of strangers, and therefore disposed to act hastily.'

Sir George waved a ham-like hand in generous acceptance of the implied apology. 'No harm done, my lord. Clement there returned at once to tell us what had happened, we came here immediately, and – and here we are,' he concluded triumphantly.

Martin looked round the hall as Sir George spoke, stopping as his eye lit on a dark corner in which stood his own servant, Clement, a man perhaps some ten years older than Martin himself, with a round face, a stubbly beard and a merry eye, which he averted hastily as Martin's gaze lit upon him.

'Yes, here you are,' said Kyme. 'But then you were on your way to see me in any case, is that not so?'

'Just so,' said Sir George. 'You yourself asked for a commission of oyer and terminer to look into this matter of the death of Master Wood, as I understand it?'

Kyme nodded vigorously. 'It's the only way to bring the murderer to justice, as I see it.'

Mr Justice Killane looked up and said in his absent-minded way, 'It is a curious fact that the young man's family also asked for a special commission. Not unusual in a civil matter, of course, but curious in a criminal case.' He looked at Kyme, and smiled again. Killane was an elderly man with long, grey hair, and eyes that seemed fixed more on the next world than this one. Many a wrongdoer, seeing those eyes, had underestimated Killane's perception, and overestimated his mercy. Martin himself had seen Killane smile in exactly that same vague way at a man whom he had just sentenced to hang.

Kyme nodded. 'The Middlehams would have acted that way, I can see that, because they seem to think that young Robert will not get a fair trial before any jury in these parts.' He stopped, seemingly about to say more, then shrugged. It was not really possible for Lord Kyme to look embarrassed, he was too used to having things his own way, but he came close to it, and looked decidedly happier when there was a sound of footsteps, and Martin looked round to see a dwarf, dressed not in cap and bells but in honest homespun, enter the room.

'Guests?' said the newcomer, bowing deeply to them all. 'Why was I not told of their arrival at once?'

'Come in, fool, if you're coming in,' said Kyme. 'These gentlemen are the special commissioners, come to look into the death of poor Master Wood. Gentlemen, this is Fortunato, one of my most trusted advisers.'

Fortunato bowed again, and smiled broadly, but his eyes had a serious look in them.

'You were both here, of course, when it happened?' asked Sir George.

'We were,' said Kyme.

'Then perhaps we might begin by hearing what you could tell us?'

'By all means.' Kyme waved Martin to a chair. 'Do you need pen and paper, Master Byrd?'

'Thank you, my man has both, your lordship.'

Clement brought paper, pen and ink, placing them all on the table in front of Martin without looking at him.

'I had arranged some small celebrations for May Day,' said Kyme. 'I like to keep up the old customs, too much change these days. Anyway, Master Wood was amongst those present, and, towards five or six o'clock –'

'Excuse me, my lord.' It was the third of the special commissioners who spoke, Mr Justice Timmons, a middle-aged man with a cheerful face. Martin knew very little about Timmons, for he had never met him until just a few days before, when the commission was appointed.

'Well?' It was clear from Kyme's tone that he did not relish being interrupted, even by a judge.

'You say Wood was among those present. Could you tell us who the others were?'

Very good, thought Martin. If Timmons thinks like that all the time, we may get to the bottom of this fairly quickly.

Kyme did not seem to share this point of view. 'Does it matter who else was, or was not, here?' he asked. 'We know –'

Killane raised a thin hand on which the blue veins stood out. 'We need to know as much as possible, my lord, if we are to investigate this matter properly. Remember if you will that none of us were present last year, so we know only so much as we are told.'

'Very well. I suppose that you have your own ways of doing these things. Let me see, there were a couple of my tenants, some of the local gentlemen who had come at my invitation, oh, I don't know. Fortunato?'

The dwarf bowed, and said, 'A couple more neighbours, come not by invitation but to ask favours at court. My lady, the servants. The villagers. Not to speak of a score of assorted vagabonds.'

'Vagabonds?' asked Sir George quickly.

Kyme waved a hand dismissively. 'Wandering musicians, jugglers, tumblers. Entertainers. A chap with a bear, I recall.'

Timmons sighed loudly. 'And this Master Wood, merchant. What sort of goods did he deal in?'

'Curiosities. Animals from Africa and the Orient. Rare gems and the like.'

Timmons shot a glance at Sir George, then asked Kyme, 'You saw his goods?'

'I bought them. A monkey and a civet – ah. Yes.' He coughed loudly.

'A monkey and a civet,' said Sir George. 'But you did say this Wood dealt in rare gems, I think? What I'm getting at is, did he have any rare gems about his person when he was at Kyme? Or any other valuables that might have been seen by a casual onlooker? Was that why he was killed, to rob him? Had you paid him for your own goods, say? Would he have any great store of money, or other easily removable valuables about him?'

'I hadn't given him any money, there had not been time. I paid Bertram, that's Wood's servant, the next day, no, the next day but one, when he left, taking Wood's body for burial in his own church. I offered to have it all done here by Father Gerald, but Bertram said that he was sure poor Wood wanted to be buried at home, so I didn't press the offer. And, in any case, I am positive that robbery was not the reason for the killing, for Wood's purse was still on his body, and had not been touched, so far as we could tell. Certainly it had plenty of money in it.'

'Who actually found the body?' Timmons again.

'His servant, Bertram. He was –'

'Nay, my lord.' Fortunato held a hand up to stop Kyme. 'You forget, it was Daisy.'

'Ah, yes. Daisy. One of the kitchen maids here,' Kyme explained. 'She stumbled over the body, quite by chance. Got a shock, as you may readily imagine. She must have found the body, become upset, and wandered off in somewhat of a daze, until she bumped into Bertram, and told him what she had found. He was with the body when the rest of us got there. He was upset, too, poor fellow.'

'And who alerted you to what had happened?' asked Sir George. 'Not this Bertram, since he was with Wood's body?'

'No, that was Daisy as well,' said Kyme, 'she appeared in the doorway there,' he waved a hand, 'she was sobbing and so forth, and as soon as we could get any sense out of her, and made out that something was wrong, I took the other gentlemen out into the courtyard, and there we found Bertram, kneeling by the side of poor Wood.'

'What o'clock would that be?' asked Sir George.

'Five? Perhaps six. About then. The meal would start about three, half past three, something like that, and it was nearly over when all the fuss started, for some of my own people had already finished and gone home.'

'And so you went outside, and found Bertram with his master, or his master's body, rather?' asked Sir George.

'Yes.'

Timmons asked, 'And had Wood been outside long, do you know?'

'No, I confess I don't know,' said Kyme, 'I didn't

notice just when it was he left the hall. People were coming and going all through the meal. You know how these things are.'

'So this Bertram could easily have gone outside before Wood was killed? He could, in fact, quite easily have been out in the yard at about the time that Wood met his death?' Timmons went on.

Kyme looked at him, frowning. 'Yes, I suppose he could have been. I had not thought about the matter quite that way, but, yes, he could.'

Martin put in, 'And why was Wood outside in the first place?'

'I don't know,' said Kyme. 'As I said, I didn't see him go out, so I couldn't hazard a guess as to when, much less why, he did so.'

'A call of nature, perhaps?' suggested Timmons.

'I don't know,' Kyme said again.

'And then there's the slightly more interesting and important question of just why this Bertram may have gone outside, in his turn,' said Timmons.

Kyme shrugged. 'Another call of nature? Does it really matter why he went outside?'

'It may do,' said Timmons quietly.

Kyme thought a moment. 'Because he may have killed Wood? Is that what you're getting at?'

'It is a possibility.'

'Rubbish. He was Wood's own man. Besides, we know very well who did it.'

'This young man,' said Sir George, consulting a memorandum he had taken from his pocket, 'this Robert Middleham?'

'Exactly.'

'And just how do you know?' asked Timmons.

Kyme looked angry. He snorted audibly, and seemed about to say something, but then he subsided as Killane held up his thin hand. 'Very well,' said Kyme. 'We know he did it, because his knife was sticking out of Wood's chest. Pretty conclusive, wouldn't you say?'

'You're certain it was his knife?' Timmons persisted.

'Certain. It was identified as his by two of my servants here, and by one of my guests into the bargain. I take it that even you won't question the word of a gentleman?'

Sir George asked, 'But did young Middleham himself admit that the knife was his?'

'When we asked him, he said that he had lost the knife, and he then stubbornly refused to answer any more of our questions.'

'When was that?' asked Timmons. 'When did you question him, or try to?'

'The day after the murder. I rode out to the Middleham house – the lad lives with his old father – along with the sheriff and a couple of his officers. Robert, as I say, would not, or could not, answer our perfectly civil questions. But he was patently upset. Guilty conscience, I should think, and rightly so.'

'You can't pre-judge the matter,' Sir George warned him.

'You can't, but I'm quite convinced. Anyway, we did it all in the correct legal form. Middleham was summoned to the Assizes, but failed to appear. Well, I was all for starting to have the statutory five proclamations made then and there, but my lord sheriff pointed out that outlawry means damn-all these days, saving your presence, gentlemen, and I had to agree. Besides, I rather think that the sheriff is some distant relation of the Middlehams. You know how it is.'

There were nods of agreement all round. Any man in a position of authority soon found that his loyalties were not by any means always clear-cut. There was always a wife's brother whose preferment had to be considered, or a wayward nephew who should have been arrested, but who could not be touched without offending one's sister.

'And so I asked the Lord Chancellor for a commission to look into the matter,' Kyme concluded.

'But Master Middleham did answer you on that day inasmuch as he maintained that he had lost his knife?' Martin asked.

Kyme looked slightly annoyed at being questioned by a mere clerk, but answered, 'Yes. As I just told you.'

'And when was that?'

Kyme sighed. 'The day after the –'

'No, your pardon, my lord. I meant to ask rather when it was that he had lost the knife, or at least when he claims to have lost it.'

'I don't know that. Since it was a lie, since he did not lose it, what can it matter when he claims to have lost it?'

'Let's leave that point for the moment, if you will,' said Sir George. 'Now, my lord, this young man, Robert Middleham was one of your guests here on May Day, is that right?'

Kyme laughed heartily. 'Scarcely that, Sir George. No, he was here without my permission or my approval, chasing one of my maids.'

Sir George frowned. 'That needs some explanation, my lord, if you would be so kind.'

Kyme came close to looking embarrassed once again, but answered readily enough. 'There's bad blood between the families of Kyme and Middleham. You must understand that the Middlehams are gentry. They have no title, but they're as old as any family in the land. Now, there was some dispute a couple of generations back, in my grandfather's time, or perhaps in his father's time, I'm not sure. I don't know what it was about, and I don't imagine the Middlehams do either, not any more. The cause is long forgotten, but the resentment lingers on. Land, most likely, field boundaries or something of that sort, they used to argue about that sort of thing in those days. Not that we don't now, of course. And then, nowadays we favour different parties at court, which makes for a certain amount of antagonism.'

'Yes, I see. And you say this young man was enamoured of one of your maids?' asked Sir George.

'Yes. That same Daisy who found Wood's body, as a matter of fact. He came sneaking round that afternoon – no, I'll be fair to the lad, he probably rode up openly enough, even though he knew how I feel about him and his family, for he's a gentleman, I'll not say otherwise, nor will I hear anyone else say otherwise – and went round to the kitchen.'

'You saw him?' asked Sir George.

'I didn't. The servants did. Ralph did.' Kyme waved towards the corner where the butler stood silently. 'Ralph told me that he was here. I was annoyed to hear it, as you may imagine.'

'But you did not face him, ask him to leave? Feeling as you did about the boy and his family, I'm surprised you didn't have your constable throw him off the estate.'

'I was all for doing just that. But my wife has a good heart, she said to let them get on with it, love's young dream, all that sort of nonsense. And then I did not really want to spoil the afternoon for everyone, not over something so trivial as that. Or so I thought at the time. I wish now that I'd followed my original inclination, had him thrown out. Master Wood would still be alive now, had I done so.'

'You cannot possibly be certain of that,' said Killane in his gentle manner.

Kyme snorted once again. 'Can I not?'

Despite the look of annoyance that his last question had produced, Martin felt compelled to ask, 'You say you did not see this Robert Middleham yourself, though, my lord?'

'As I said. Ralph did, though. And Fortunato did.'

'Indeed?'

'Indeed, Master Clerk.' Fortunato bowed low.

'And did you also see him leave?'

Fortunato frowned. 'Not I.'

'Did anyone?'

Fortunato shrugged, and looked a question at Kyme.

'I didn't see him come, or go either, as I've told you,' said Kyme, in a more reasonable tone. 'Nor did any of the other servants mention it. Not that I thought to ask them, of course.'

'So there's no telling even whether the young man was still here when Master Wood met his death?' asked Timmons. Martin looked at him gratefully, glad to have been spared the necessity of questioning Kyme further himself.

'It's clear that he must have been,' said Kyme triumphantly, 'since he killed him.'

Even Sir George was stirred into protesting at this, while Killane held up his hand again as if he meant to speak, then let it fall without saying anything.

'Well, just who else do you imagine did it?' demanded

Kyme. 'It was his knife, he didn't deny that – couldn't deny it, it was his, no doubt of that – so who else could it have been?'

'But you said, for instance, that you had a troupe of wandering players in the house,' said Timmons.

Killane put in, 'In my experience, which is considerable, such gentry are not particularly honest even at the best of times. It is not entirely out of the question that one of them may have stolen this young man's knife, for they are skilled in petty theft, picking pockets and the like, and then murdered Wood for his purse.'

'Ah, but then his purse was not taken, or even tampered with, so that can't have been the cause.'

Killane smiled. 'Perhaps there was not the time to rob him. This girl who found Wood's body may well have disturbed the man who killed him, causing him to flee without completing his task.'

'That is a possibility I hadn't thought of,' said Kyme. 'And, were it true, I'd rather welcome it, do you know? Young Middleham is at least a gentleman, whatever else he is, and whatever the quarrel between our families may be. But then, if he were innocent, why should he refuse to appear at the Assizes when summoned?'

Sir George stirred. 'I understand that the Assizes were in October of last year?'

Kyme nodded.

'This Robert Middleham failed to appear,' Sir George went on. 'That's not uncommon in these lawless days, I regret to say. Indeed, it happens all the time. But then my lord Kemp has not one, but two, requests for a special commission to look into the matter.'

Kyme nodded again. 'The Middlehams seem to think that Robert would find a jury prejudiced against him.'

He hesitated. 'I will not say that they are completely wrong about that.' He paused, shrugged, and went on, 'You gentlemen are men of the world, you know how matters stand. Were it not difficult always to obtain impartial judgements, there would be no work for men such as yourself.'

'Quite so,' said Sir George. 'Now, if your lordship will excuse us, we must be on our way. It's an hour or so to Norwich, and we have yet to arrange accommodation for ourselves, not to speak of seeing the sheriff to settle the date and place for the hearing, though that may well have to wait until tomorrow.'

'But surely you won't think of going on? Do you not intend to stay here?' Kyme asked. 'I have plenty of room, and you'll be more than welcome.'

Sir George looked at his two colleagues, who did not seem averse to the idea of staying. 'Very kind of you, my lord.'

Kyme looked round. 'Ralph, where are you? Ah, could you make ready some rooms for our guests? I take it your servants will be happy to sleep in here, Sir George, along with my own?'

'Oh, they'll be perfectly happy. I'll have something to say if they complain,' said Sir George. 'Martin here should have his own room, of course.'

Kyme did not look as if Martin's welfare were of the slightest concern to him, but he nodded at Ralph. 'See to that as well, then, would you, Ralph? Now, gentlemen, Ralph will show you your rooms, and I look forward to seeing you at dinner. We dine around three.' Kyme got up and left the hall, with Fortunato marching after him.

Ralph said, 'Gentlemen, if you'll follow me.' He looked at Martin almost with contempt, and added, 'If you'll wait here a moment, Master Clerk, I'll see what can be done in the way of a room for you,' and he led the way out, the three Justices following.

Martin now had a chance to look properly at Clement. He favoured him with a long stare, which Clement withstood for as long as he decently could – and it was not long at that – and then he looked down at his shabby boots, and asked, 'You were not treated so very badly this morning, I trust, master? Not hurt, or roughly handled, or anything?'

'Oh, I wasn't treated too badly, all things considered,' said Martin.

'No? Good, I'm glad to hear that.'

'No. I was put in a cellar too small to stand upright in, but what of that? True, it stank, and the walls were dripping with God knows what, much of which is on my new coat, as you can plainly see. But apart from that, not too badly at all, thank you.'

'Master, there were five men-at-arms,' said Clement earnestly. 'What could I do against five? All that would have happened would have been that we both ended up in the dungeon, and what use would that have been, I ask you? That was why I thought it wiser to ride off before they caught up with us, and tell Sir George what was happening.'

'Oh, it was. Much wiser. Very much wiser. I only wish you'd told me what you proposed to do. I'd have galloped off with you, instead of sitting there thinking they'd be friendly, if not actually helpful. And that's another thing. Where's my horse?'

'He's well. He's in the stable. Harry, the constable, took care of him. Nice fellow, Harry, isn't he? Looks as if he'd be a good drinking companion. In fact, I'm seeing him later, we're off to the village inn. Looks the sort of chap who likes a good laugh. Though I fancy he was a bit disappointed that you weren't an outlaw.'

'Why, for Heaven's sake?'

'Well, if Lord Kyme had hanged you, Harry would have got your horse and other bits and pieces, wouldn't he?'

'I'm extremely sorry to have to disappoint him. I trust that he'll eventually recover from the blow.'

'Oh, I'm sure he will,' said Clement cheerfully. 'It's an ill wind, as they say. And Harry seems the sort of man who doesn't flinch under a bit of bad luck. Tough, Harry is. Like me. Old dogs for hard roads. As for that other little matter, I thought you were following me, I really did. I thought at least you would have had sense enough for that. Still, that's all behind us, now. And we've landed on our feet here, all right.' He waved a hand to indicate the spacious hall and the door to the kitchen, which stood a little ajar, and through which smells of cooking were beginning to waft.

'Yes,' said Martin, who, try as he might, could never be angry with Clement for very long. 'I fancy Lord Kyme's hospitality will be on a lavish scale.' He was about to say more when Ralph came back into the hall.

'Master Clerk, I think I've found a suitable room for you, if you'll be kind enough to come this way,' and Ralph took them out into the courtyard, crossed to one of the newer wings, and he threw open a little door. 'There you are.'

Martin stepped past him and looked inside. The room was small, and was obviously used as a storeroom in the general run of things, for there were old wicker baskets, blankets and all manner of oddments piled against the walls. The only light came from a tiny window high in one wall, reminding Martin irresistibly of his recent sojourn in the dungeon.

'It's not big,' said Ralph, coming close to sounding apologetic, 'but it is at least private.'

'Is it big enough for two?' asked Clement, pushing past Martin for a better look.

Ralph looked at him in some surprise. 'I thought you'd be sleeping in the great hall. The Kyme servants all do that.'

Clement looked aghast at this suggestion. 'But I'm Master Byrd's personal servant. I must accompany him wherever he goes, no two ways about that.' He looked round the room, then said, 'Big enough, master. Plenty big enough for the two of us,' and he bowed elaborately to Ralph by way of thanking him.

Ralph cast a single, scornful glance at him, then left without saying anything.

Clement made a rude gesture in the direction of Ralph's back, shut the door carefully, and began rummaging amongst the various bits and pieces in the room.

'If we pile these blankets up, here, and here, that'll make us a tolerable bed, master. It isn't exactly sweet smelling in here, but we can always open the door later, if you really think we need to, and if it isn't too draughty, of course. And if there's onions for supper, it won't matter anyway.'

Martin, who had experienced Clement's love of onions at second hand before today, shuddered. He said, 'I rather think you shocked Ralph there. He fully expected you to curl up in the straw in the great hall.'

Clement, who had a chamber to himself back home, said, 'A bit old fashioned, all that sort of thing, don't

46

you think? It may have been very well at one time, but now?'

'I get the impression that Lord Kyme is a bit old fashioned himself, in the best possible sense, mark you. Keeping up the old customs, and all that sort of thing.'

'He was not over-civil to you, master. Nor was that butler fellow, who rather fancies himself, though I'm damned if I can see why. And are your own people not gentry?'

Martin laughed. 'My father is a Knight of the Bath. And that was in lieu of a pension from the King, or so he always maintains. No, we cannot quite be classed with my lord of Kyme.'

Clement stretched luxuriously on the heap of blankets. 'This is better than a poxy inn.'

'It is, indeed,' agreed Martin.

'And has my lord got the right of the matter?' asked Clement. 'Did this young man, Robert Middleham, kill the merchant, think you?'

'It's too soon to tell that. That's why we, Sir George and the others, I mean, are here, when all's said and done. It does look very much as if the young man may have done it. And yet there are objections.'

'Are there?'

'Oh, yes.'

'But what about the young man failing to appear at the Assizes?' asked Clement. 'Is that not a sign of guilt?'

Martin laughed. 'Not necessarily. The sheriff appoints the jurors, and the sheriff has to live with Lord Kyme, as do the jurors. Anyone who is not a friend of Kyme's, or of Suffolk's, therefore, cannot be sure that his case will be judged without partiality.'

'Yet the young man's family must have some friend at court, though, to ask for the special commission on their behalf?'

'Probably young Jack of Norfolk, I imagine,' said Martin. 'He leads what might be called the opposite faction to that of Suffolk, though most of the great men are looking out for their own interests.'

'As is only natural.'

'I only hope we're allowed to pursue the matter without interference,' said Martin.

'What sort of interference?'

'Political, Clement. The Lord Chancellor can move the entire matter to London with a writ of supersedeas.'

Clement was puzzled. 'And why should he do that?'

'Oh, if the young man's family think it likely that he will be judged guilty, and so make issue with Lord Kemp. Or if his enemies think he's likely to go free. Or if Kemp himself thinks something should be hushed up, which is not unlikely these days.'

Clement lowered his voice. 'This business of the Lord Chancellor wanting to keep things hushed up, that's something I can understand right enough. After all, if he hasn't got plenty to hide, who has? When you're in his place, you'll have to do that sort of thing every day. Don't worry, I'll be there to advise you as to what must be kept quiet. But this other business, writs here and writs there, according as the young man's family make interest at court, or Lord Kyme does, as the case may be. Does justice then go to the man with the longest purse, as it is said?'

'To the man with the most friends at court, or, rather, the man with the most powerful friends at court.'

'And that's Kyme? Or Suffolk? The young man had best look out.'

'I don't know. A year ago, perhaps. But Suffolk has his own enemies, men who would not be sorry to see him go. He's been obliged to speak on his own behalf, in his own defence, to be blunt, before Parliament. And there was a petition of indictment brought against him, alleging this and that, I know not, only lately. So things look unsettled, to say the least. If Suffolk falls, who shall stand? That alone might bring a writ of supersedeas.' Martin shrugged again.

'There was a tale that the King had banished him. Suffolk, I mean.'

Martin laughed. 'Aye, for five years. But the King seems to have made that decision only to keep Suffolk's enemies quiet. It's certain that Suffolk's still at large.'

'Made up to a Duke one year, banished the next, eh?'

'The vagaries and vicissitudes of public life, good Clement. Be thankful you're not a great man. The bigger they are, the harder they fall.'

'A bit of a disappointment, though, master. Like a cockerel who's clawed his way to the top of the dunghill, only to find himself in the stew-pot with a bunch of leeks up his arse.'

'I'm sure my lord Suffolk would appreciate the simile.'

Clement scratched his head. 'I wonder if it's almost three yet?'

'And why? What has the time of day to do with Suffolk, or with similes, then?'

Clement looked puzzled. 'Why, nothing. What should the time of day have to do with Lord Suffolk, or yet with similes? But three o'clock is when my lord Kyme is pleased to dine, or so he said. I could do with my dinner.'

'So could I, now you mention the subject,' said Martin. 'It has been a long day, and a somewhat tiring one. I must confess to being pleased that Easter is over, though even then my lord Kyme does not strike me as the sort of man who keeps Lent too rigorously. There may be advantages in being here, when I think the matter over.'

'Yes, the food and drink should be excellent.'

'Yes, that too. But I was thinking more of the chance that it affords us to get busy and discover the truth of this matter of Master Wood's death.'

'Get busy?' There was a cautious note in Clement's voice.

'Yes. Since we're here, we can talk to those who were present at last year's festivities, or to many of them, at least. That way we may be able to get this sorted out before Kemp can think of changing his mind.'

'When you say "we", I take it you refer to Sir George and the other two? I mean, they are the Justices, after all. We are only very small fish in the pond, master.'

'We. All of us. For, mark you, good Clement, you and I are as much officers of the court as Sir George or the others. Or very nearly so. That being the case, we must – all of us – do everything we can to bring the matter to a successful conclusion.'

'If by some mischance the culprit is one of those wandering players, then we'll never find him.' Clement did not seem too bothered by this possibility. 'Those fellows travel miles in a day, even when they've nothing to hide. When they have – well, like I say, we'll just never find them.'

'All the more reason why we should be diligent. For mark you well, Clement, if it was one of those vagabonds, then you and I could be travelling for the rest of our days to track him down, eating what we can get, when we can get it, and sleeping in those poxy inns of which you spoke.'

'You're quite earnest, aren't you?'

Martin nodded, and Clement looked horrified. 'And now,' said Martin cheerfully, 'let's see about some dinner.'

Three

Clement pushed his way into the crowded kitchen, turned inside the door and waved a hand towards Martin. 'Come in, Master Byrd, no standing on ceremony here,' he called out loudly.

Martin went in rather hesitantly, conscious of the fact that everyone was looking at him, a natural response to any stranger, but especially to a stranger associated with the law.

'This is Martha,' Clement went on, waving at a buxom woman. 'I introduced myself in here last night.'

Martha blushed, and Martin, wondering just what form the introduction might have taken, for he knew Clement well, sat down before a breakfast of bread and cheese. 'Please join us,' he told Martha, waving a hand at an empty seat. 'I wanted a chance to talk to you, to all the servants, that is to say, and this is as good a time as any to start.'

Martha's expression turned to outright fear at this statement, but Clement gave her his famous reassuring smile, the one that had never let him down yet, especially with women, or so he claimed, and poured a generous mug of beer for her.

Somewhat reassured by this courtesy, Martha gave a little smile, and asked Martin, 'Am I right in thinking that you're the clerk to the Justices, sir?'

Martin nodded.

'Well, sir,' Martha went on, 'I can see that you would be wanting to clear up this sad business of Master Wood's death, but I can't for the life of me think what you imagine I may have had to do with it. I know nothing at all about it, I can promise you –'

Martin held a hand up to silence her, and said, 'The thing is, you see, Martha, when Master Wood met his death, Lord Kyme and the other gentry were all in the great hall, so they could not possibly have seen anything that may have happened in the courtyard. But the door there, that gives on to the courtyard, would be standing open, and people would be coming and going in and out all day long, when there was a special meal being served. So that anyone in here would have been far more likely to have seen anything that went on out in the courtyard than anyone in the great hall would.'

Martha's look of uncertainty turned to one of sheer terror. 'But, sir, if any of us had seen anything, then I'm sure we would have told his lordship all about it at the time. And, although the door probably was open, just as you say, though I couldn't speak as to that, then in any event we'd have been too busy to look out, just to pass the time, as you might say, and then as like as not we'd have come and gone through the house itself, through the buttery, you know –'

'Yes, I see. Apart from the unfortunate death of Master Wood, is there anything else that you remember about that day? What were you yourself doing, can you tell me?'

Martha considered this carefully. 'Well, there was a great deal of work to be done. It was a warmish day, I remember that. So, yes, now I come to think about it, you're right, the door to the yard stood open. And the

place was crowded, as I remember, a lot of those vaga-
bond musicians and jugglers and what have you. If you
ask me, I dare say it was one of them that did it. Nasty lot,
them strolling players, and you can say what you like. If
you want to know what I think, begging your pardon, sir,
I think you should ask them about it. Mark my words,
they'll know all about it.'

'We had already thought of that,' said Martin, 'and I'm
sure that the Justices would consider that to be the most
likely explanation, as anyone would. But the only thing
wrong with that is that the knife belonged to this young
Master Middleham. That much seems certain beyond
any doubt.'

Martha looked concerned. 'But then he must have lost
it, sir.' She leaned over the table towards Martin, and said
confidentially, 'I do hear say that's what he told my lord
sheriff, that he'd lost the knife, and had no idea at all as
to where it might have gone. And I can swear to you that
he's not the kind of young man to tell any sort of a lie.
And much less would he kill another man in that way. A
very pleasant, harmless young man, sir.'

'And did you see Robert Middleham yourself that day
at all?'

'That I did, sir. He came by the kitchen door, and
paused outside, shy like, as if wondering whether he dare
come inside. Pretty much as you yourself were doing a
while ago.'

Martin flushed, while Clement grinned broadly, and
winked at Martha.

'And what then?' asked Martin, when he had managed
to recover some of his composure.

Martha went on, 'He called out to me, passing the time
of day, like, for he always spoke to me, there's no sort of

edge to him at all, and he asked me, "Martha, is Daisy there?" just like that. And I said, "Yes, sir, I'll tell her you're here", and so I did. Daisy, sir, being one of the maids, you see. But I suppose you'll know that already?' She paused, and sighed. 'What you may not know as yet, though, sir, is that Master Middleham was fond of Daisy. Very fond of her, in fact.'

'And is this Daisy here now?' asked Martin.

Martha looked round the crowded kitchen. 'No, sir. Not just at the moment.'

'I'm sure we'll get the chance to talk to her later. But please go on with your account.'

'Well, sir, there's really not all that much more to tell. I told Daisy that Master Middleham was here asking for her, and her face lit up, as it always did when he called to see her, and she asked me to look after whatever it was she was doing at the time, and then she ran out to see him.'

'And did you see any more of the two of them after that? Later that day, perhaps?'

'No, sir. I was very busy in here, as you'll realize.'

'And do you by any chance happen to recall whether Master Middleham had a knife hanging at his belt when he called at the kitchen door?'

Martha shot a horrified look at him. 'You mean the knife that was –' and she broke off, and flung her apron over her face.

'No, no,' said Martin hastily, looking round to see whether they were attracting any undue attention. Fortunately there was nobody close at hand at the moment to witness Martha's discomposure. 'No, not *that* knife, of course I didn't mean that, for he claims that he had lost it, and we can't say otherwise. I just meant to ask whether you noticed if he had any sort of a knife at all hanging at his belt.'

Martha wiped her eyes and sniffed loudly. 'Lord, sir, I couldn't say. I never noticed. It isn't the sort of thing a body would notice, now is it?'

'No, of course not.' He went on, 'I hope I'm not sounding too pompous or anything of that sort, but did you never think it strange that this Master Middleham, a gentleman as I understand it, should pay court to a kitchen maid?'

Martha, now fully recovered, beamed at him. 'Oh, I can see that anyone might think like that, not having met Daisy, but when you see her for yourself, you'll not think it strange at all, sir. Lovely, she is. I understand they first met quite by chance, Master Robert riding by as Daisy was coming back from the village on some errand. Romantic, isn't it? Like one of those ballads the minstrels sing. And as for her being a kitchen maid, why, there's many a gentleman as has married his cook,' and she sighed, perhaps at the thought of what might have been.

'Cook indeed,' said Clement, 'why, there's many a gentleman as has married –'

'That'll do,' Martin told him. 'And did you know that there was some bad blood between the young man's family and Lord Kyme?'

'Lord love us, sir, yes, of course. But we had no notion of what had caused that, and I don't think his lordship could tell you either, if you was to ask him. Some old quarrel or another. But the young man, sir, he was so pleasant and likeable. And Daisy's such a nice girl, so we were all so very happy for them. And, of course, now –' and Martha sighed, and left it at that.

'So, Martha, you didn't think to say or do anything

about Master Middleham being here that day?'

Martha gave him a conspiratorial smile. 'What his lordship didn't know wouldn't hurt him, would it now, sir? That's what we all thought. Of course, had we known there'd be all this fuss, that might've been a different matter altogether, but we weren't to know. How could we?'

'Of course not. And you didn't see anything more of Daisy and Master Middleham that day, once they had met in here and gone outside together? You don't know where they may have gone?'

'No, sir.'

'Then when did you next see either one of them?'

'Well, sir, Daisy, now. I didn't see anything more of her all that afternoon, not until there was all the fuss and palaver over Master Wood being found.' Martha shuddered. 'Then, of course, I more or less had to take her under my wing, as you might say, for she was proper upset, as you can imagine, what with finding the poor man like that. As was my lady, or so Janet, that's her maid, told me. Floods of tears, Janet told me. And swooning, and that. Proper took, she was, or so Janet told me. Though of course I couldn't speak as to the truth of that, for I didn't have anything to do with my lady myself, as you'll realize. Busy enough with poor little Daisy, I was, in all conscience.'

'When did young Middleham come calling? What o'clock?'

'Well, the meal had just decently started, I do know that.'

'And Daisy found Wood's body towards the end of the meal, is that right?'

Martha shuddered again, but nodded agreement.

'So that means the meal had run its full course, more or less? Then we can allow, say, two hours by the clock? Three, perhaps?'

Martha nodded again. 'Nearer three, I should say, sir, for it was a big meal, a special one.'

'I see. And you saw nothing at all of Master Middleham, I take it, beyond speaking to him at the kitchen door?'

'No, sir.'

'So you couldn't speak as to when it was that he actually left Kyme, for instance?'

'No, sir, I'm very sorry. I haven't seen hide nor hair of him at all, from that day to this.'

'He's not called on Daisy since?'

'Oh, no, sir. He'd not dare, not the way things are. His lordship would have him thrown in the dungeon, like as not, if he dared to show his face here just now.'

Martin winced. 'Well, thank you for talking to me like this, Martha. You've been very helpful. And don't forget, if I, or Sir George, or any of the others should need to ask you any further questions, don't you be afraid at all, just answer them honestly, as you have my questions today, and everything will be well.' He stood up and smiled at her. 'Thank you for the breakfast. And now, Clement, we had best seek out Sir George, or we'll get the rough edge of his tongue.'

They found Sir George and the other two members of the commission seated in the great hall. There was no sign of either Lord or Lady Kyme.

'Ah, there you are at last. I trust you don't expect any breakfast. It's the middle of the day, man.' Sir George brushed a few stray bread crumbs from his chin, pushed his chair back and stood up.

'I have already breakfasted, Sir George. In the kitchen.'

'Oh? And why there?'

'I thought it might be as well to question the servants concerning Master Wood's death.'

'And again, why?' There was no truculence in the question, Sir George was just genuinely puzzled.

'Because Lord Kyme and the other gentlemen were in here when it happened, and hence could see nothing. On the other hand, the servants were in and out of the kitchen, in and out of here, in and out of the courtyard, for all we know. One of them may well have seen something which could have a bearing on the matter.'

'Nonsense, they'd have told Lord Kyme straight away had they done so. Made a fuss, raised the hue and cry then and there.'

'That's what they told me,' Martin had to admit.

'There you are, then. Waste of time.' He looked at his two colleagues. 'Well, now, gentlemen, I think that our first task must be to go into Norwich today, see the sheriff, and arrange a time and a place for the formal hearing. Martin, there's no need for you to come with us for that, so would you take your man and go see this Robert Middleham?'

'I will, Sir George.'

'Don't say anything to scare the lad, just make sure that he is willing to appear before us, and that he understands what it's all about. He should be willing enough, since he, or at any rate his family, asked for a special commission in the first place, but it's as well to make certain. And if you possibly could get some sort of a story from him that would be useful. I wouldn't for one moment expect him to make a full confession to you, or anything of that sort, of course, but, if we have his version of events noted down, then that may help us to get things settled in our minds before the hearing, let us know what sort of questions we need to put to him, and so forth. Does that sound reasonable?'

'Indeed, Sir George.' Martin led the way outside.

'A better day,' observed Clement, nodding at the sky, in which the sun now shone brightly.

'Aye. We don't know where this young Middleham lives, but Ralph may.'

Clement nodded, and put his head round the kitchen door. In reply to his question, Martha told them that Ralph was in the buttery, and pointed the way.

They found Ralph busy checking the stores, but he condescended to break off when they asked where Middleham lived. The Middleham estate was a short half-hour's ride to the south-west, the opposite direction to that taken by Sir George and the others, said Ralph, and a fit man could walk the distance in a little over an hour.

'I think I'll ride,' said Martin, 'my horse is getting fat.'

'I'll ride too,' said Clement hastily, lest there should be any silly misunderstanding on this point.

'Then I'll go with you to the stables, and point the way,' said Ralph. 'I could do with some fresh air myself.' He took them back through the kitchen, and set off across the courtyard.

'I understand it was out here that Master Wood was killed,' said Martin, looking round the yard.

Ralph altered direction very slightly, and after a dozen paces he stopped at a spot near the stables, and pointed to the ground. 'Just here it was that we found him,' he said.

Martin stood very close to the spot which Ralph had indicated, and looked carefully round the courtyard. On the far side of it, one of the scullions was scraping out a pan by the kitchen door, for the benefit of a couple of hens and an aggressive cockerel. On this side, a couple of men were leading horses out of the stable, while just inside the stable door a sturdy blacksmith was shoeing another horse.

Martin said, 'Whoever killed Wood was surely taking a very great risk, doing so out here and in broad daylight?'

'It was late afternoon,' said Ralph. 'You can see where the sun would be, there were some deep shadows cast by the walls. And it was a sunnier spring last year than it has been this, so the shadows in the corners would have been darker by contrast. And all the kitchens are at the other side of the yard, as you see, and all the stable lads and others were at the feast.'

'Even so, it was a risk. What if there had been someone in the stables? Or if someone had happened to look out of the kitchen door? That's not so unlikely.'

'They were busy serving the meal, you must remember. Too busy to stand gawping. But, yes, I take your meaning.' Ralph stared towards the kitchen, his brow furrowed in thought. 'Ah, yes, I have it now. Those tumblers and the like had a wagon with them, I remember, and it was left here. And then Master Wood's own cart was here as well, by the stables, but on the house side, considering it from where we stand here. That was it, the body was hidden away as it were behind the two carts, so Master Wood and whoever killed him could not have been seen at all from the house.'

'Yes, I see that. Tell me,' asked Martin, 'what sort of a man was Wood?'

'Master Wood?' Ralph considered the question carefully. 'He was a merchant. What more can I say? As honest as any merchant, I dare say. God rest his soul.'

'Amen to that. But what was he like as a man? Was he married, say?'

'No.' Ralph sounded certain.

'You are quite sure?'

'Quite sure. No wife, no child. I can tell you that for certain because I happen to know that his man, Bertram, was also his heir. It's Bertram who runs the business these days.'

'That same Bertram who was bending over Wood's body when you and the others came out here?'

'Yes, the same. Terribly upset, he was, as you may imagine. After all, Master Wood must have been like a father to him, leaving him the business and all.'

'Yes,' said Martin thoughtfully, 'it must have come as a considerable shock to him. But to return to Master Wood. Was he a big man?'

'About my own size, perhaps a touch taller. Broad shoulders, dark hair, good looking in a rough way.'

'A man who could take care of himself, would you say?'

Ralph laughed. 'Aye, he looked as if he would give a good account of himself in a brawl. I'd not like to cross him.'

'And was he a likeable man?'

'As to that, I can hardly say.'

'Oh, come now! You must surely have formed some idea of his character.'

'No, I could not honestly tell you. I got on all right with him, when I talked to him, but then he came here so infrequently that I could not truthfully say I knew him very well at all. He'd not been here for, what, two years? Perhaps three, since his last visit. It was a bit awkward for him, of course, here at Kyme, for he was a merchant, so not of my lord's class, yet he was not on the same level as the farm labourers and village churls. I suppose you could say he was nearest to myself in that respect, but I don't have the time to stand gossiping, so Master Wood mostly kept to himself. He talked with Bertram a good deal, of course, so he wasn't exactly just sitting in a corner on his own, but you couldn't say that he mixed with anyone in particular in the house on his visits.'

'So he had no close friends, or even any particular acquaintance here at Kyme?'

'Not at all.'

'And you say he'd not been here for some three years in any event?'

'That's so,' said Ralph. 'Why all the questions?'

'To find out what sort of man he was,' said Martin. 'Then we may be able to work out what sort of man would want to kill him.'

'My lord's worked that out already.' There was a note of irony in Ralph's voice which could not be missed.

'You disagree with my lord's opinion?'

'Why would this young man kill a merchant he did not know? A man might kill to rob, yet Wood's purse was intact.' He gave a short laugh. 'True, the young man did seem to suffer from lovesickness, but the madness which that induces is usually confined to writing bad verses, or baying at the moon. No, he had no reason to kill Wood, therefore any reasonable man, any man not prejudiced by some old quarrel with the young man's entire family, must surely judge that he did not do so.'

'And yet his knife was used to do it?'

Ralph stared at the ground in silence for a time. 'That does tell against him, I must allow,' he said at length. 'And yet, if the knife had not been known for his, would anyone have thought for a moment that he had done it?

What would the natural conclusion have been, think you? That one of the strolling players had done it, to rob Master Wood, but had been disturbed before he could take the purse. And that, I believe, is exactly the way of it. Whoever did kill Wood either stole the young man's knife, or more likely found it after he had lost it, for young Middleham himself claims that he did lose it.'

'That is one explanation. Tell me, how was the body laid on the ground? On the back, or the belly?'

'Face down.'

'At full length?'

Ralph considered this. 'No, he was somewhat huddled up, I should say. Face to the ground, but doubled up, as it were.'

'And where was the knife? Back or front?'

'Front, in the centre of his chest. He must have died instantly, rest his soul.'

'And where is it now? Anywhere at Kyme?'

'The knife, you mean? Yes, my lord instructed me to guard it safely, lest it be needed as evidence.'

'So you have it now? May I see it?'

Ralph frowned. 'I suppose you have your own ways of doing things. Very well, Master Clerk, you are here in an official capacity, so I expect there's no harm in it. This way, if you please,' and he turned and set off back towards the house.

Martin and Clement followed him up a narrow stairway and into what was evidently Ralph's own sparsely furnished room, where he went over to a heavy oak chest, produced a large key from somewhere about his person, opened the chest and took out an object wrapped in a piece of cloth.

'There,' and Ralph handed it to Martin, who unwrapped

the cloth gingerly to reveal a knife, the whole length of the blade stained a rusty colour.

Martin looked at the knife closely. The hilt was of horn, with silver wire round it, and there was an oval carnelian set in the top. To make identification even easier, the initials 'RM' had been cut into the stone.

'Distinctive enough,' said Martin, showing the knife to Clement.

'Aye,' said Ralph heavily. 'There's no mistaking whose it is. I could wish there had been.'

Martin wrapped the knife up again, and handed it back to Ralph, who locked it away again in the chest.

'Thank you for letting me see it,' said Martin, 'though it doesn't tell me much, beyond the fact that it could hardly be confused with a more ordinary knife. But now we must be on our way.'

Ralph walked back to the stables with them, watched as they saddled their horses, then accompanied them to the bridge and pointed the way out to them. 'I must get back to work,' he said, 'or I'd walk part of the way. But you cannot mistake the path, and if you chanced to do so, there are plenty of people about in the fields and woods.'

As they went through the village, Clement, who had been wriggling with suppressed excitement, asked, 'Did you mark what Ralph said about Wood's servant also being his heir, master?'

'I did, but I thought it best to say nothing. Ralph evidently saw nothing remarkable about it, which probably means that nobody else has done so either.'

'If a man knew that he would inherit the whole of another man's estate in any event, then there would be no need to lift his purse, would there, master? For it would be his anyway, with none to argue as to the rights and wrongs of it.'

'A point which had not escaped me,' said Martin. 'Mr Justice Timmons did say something as to Bertram's having been out in the yard when Wood was killed, but it passed unremarked at the time.'

'I recall it.'

'Now, I could not see why a servant should wish to kill the man who paid his wages, and thereby bring about the loss of his place and his livelihood, so I thought no more about it. But this piece of news throws a new light on the matter.'

'Aye, it might serve to explain the full purse right enough. And the killing of the merchant to boot. Love and money, master, the twin causes of all upsets in this life. And money the greater of the two.'

'And yet,' said Martin, 'if a man who was to inherit another man's estate wanted to kill that man, but make it look as if he had not, would he not be better to take the other man's purse, so as to make it look as if robbery pure and simple were at the back of the killing? To disarm the suspicion of himself that must inevitably follow?'

Clement thought this over. 'True, but perhaps he was not thinking straight? And then, if it was this Bertram, he'd already used another man's knife to do the job, perhaps he thought that was more than enough to throw suspicion on the knife's owner? As, indeed, it has done. Or did do, until two old hounds such as ourselves happened on the right scent.'

Martin shook his head. 'But then we must ask why did he wait until the two of them were at Kyme, if he'd planned it all so carefully? For all that Ralph insisted that the act would have been hidden by carts, or by deep shadows, or aught else, it was none the less a terrible risk for the murderer, out there in broad daylight, and the house full of people.'

'That's certainly true.'

'If it were Bertram who did it, why not do it when the two of them were alone, in some remote spot? If he'd done that, and then claimed that it was done by thieves, that he himself had only just managed to escape with his life, would that not be more plausible? The only reason for doing it here at Kyme would be just that there were plenty of strangers here, the strolling players and what-not, and thus suspicion might more easily fall on them. And if Wood's purse had been taken, then suspicion would indeed have fallen on them, and very understand-ably so. But, since the purse was left, then it was not robbery, and hence suspicion must fall on Bertram, as being the only man who gained by Wood's death. And, as to the knife, he could surely not rely on finding, or even stealing, another man's knife to do the killing?'

Clement considered this in silence for a time. 'All very true, if he had planned it. It may have been that he had not planned it, then.'

'But, in that case, why, suddenly, without planning it, kill a man whose goods you knew you were going to inherit in any case? Unless –'

'Yes?'

'If Wood had recently announced that he was about to marry, shall we say. In that event, he'd change his will in favour of his wife, or any children that he might sire. That could well change things, make a man act hastily to retrieve the situation. H'mm. But in that event, would it not have been as well to wait until they were on their way back, to choose a lonely spot, to make up some tale of outlawry such as I have suggested? That means the matter must have been very pressing. One thing is certain, to me at least, and that is that it was not planned, but done hastily, on the spur of the moment.'

'Or planned carefully so as to look that way, master?'

Martin stared at Clement without replying, then rode on for a time in thought.

They did not hurry, wanting to make the most of the day, but even so it was only a short ride to the Middleham lands, and they soon came to an old manor house, not so large or so grand as Kyme, but a nice, comfortable old place none the less. A word with a passing labourer confirmed that this was the Middleham house, and they rode up to the door. Clement knocked, and the door was opened by an old man, with a very red face and an alert eye. A couple of dogs lurked at his heels, and dogs and man alike regarded Clement with some suspicion.

Four

Keeping a wary eye on the dogs, Martin followed Mr Middleham into the house. A middle-aged woman who looked remarkably like Martha was clearing the table, and Mr Middleham asked her, 'Margaret, would you find Robert, and ask him to come here?'

The woman nodded, left the room and a moment later a youth of around nineteen or twenty, as far as Martin could judge, good looking enough, except that his mouth had an peevish twist to it, came in.

'Robert, these are the special commissioners.'

'Hardly that, sir,' Martin hastened to explain. 'I'm secretary to their honours, nothing more than that. They have sent me to ask whether Master Robert is willing to appear before them in Norwich, as soon as they can arrange matters satisfactorily.'

'Oh, yes. He'll appear.' It was old Mr Middleham who spoke. 'After all, it was me asked Lord Kemp to send out someone with a bit of integrity to look into this business. Robert's nothing to hide. When d'you think it'll be?'

'That's not settled as yet, sir. The head of the special commission, Sir George Maryon, is trying to arrange a venue, and a convenient time, for the formal hearing. He has asked me to come here to see you, to let you know how matters stand. And also to make some preliminary enquiries, should Master Middleham feel able to answer them.'

'Of course, you'll want to question him. Robert, take them out into the garden.'

Robert nodded, and led the way into a little orchard of gnarled old trees at the back of the house.

'First of all, was your father right when he said that you'd be happy to answer my questions?' asked Martin. 'I should tell you that I can't compel you to speak to me, though the Justices can, of course, later.'

'Oh, yes. I'm more than happy to talk in less formal surroundings than the court, and I have, as father puts it, nothing to hide, so ask what you will, and I'll do my best to answer.' The reply came at once.

'If you've nothing to hide, why not appear at the Assizes?'

Robert laughed, his rather sulky face lighting up. 'You honestly know so little of how things stand here? My family has some longstanding dispute with Lord Kyme. And the sheriff is Suffolk's man, which means Kyme's man. And thus the jury are the same. Kyme's men, to a man, so to speak.'

Martin nodded. 'That's what I understood to be the case. So it was the fear that you'd not get a fair trial that kept you away?'

'Knowledge, not fear. That's why father insisted on petitioning Lord Kemp for this special commission of yours. To ensure that I get a fair hearing, if at all possible. My father has some friends at court, perhaps not so grand nor so powerful as Suffolk, but useful none the less, and they had a word with the Lord Chancellor. And your being here is the result.'

'That's clear enough, then. And it agrees with what we've already heard. Tell me, did you know that Lord Kyme had done the selfsame thing, and petitioned Lord

Kemp for a special commission?'

'Did he, now?' It was evidently the first that Robert had heard of it. He frowned, looking more like a petulant schoolboy than ever. 'No, I'd not heard that. And it's very odd, now that I do come to know of it. Why on earth should he have wanted to do that?'

'He claims that he did it because his sole interest is in seeing justice done. He says he wants the murderer brought to book, and that is not possible so long as you refuse to appear at the Assizes.'

Robert's frown vanished, and he laughed out loud. 'Your pardon, Master Byrd. It's not you or your conversation that I find amusing, but the notion that Kyme wants justice. If he wanted justice, then why did he accuse me in the first place? And why does he still insist that I appear before a court, even before a relatively honest one such as yours? No, what Kyme wants is – what can I call it? Revenge, perhaps. Spite, a desire to hit at my family by hitting at me, that's why he's doing this.'

'He is quite convinced that you did it.'

'But the whole idea's ridiculous!' Robert said angrily. 'I'd nothing whatever to do with the death of this merchant. I'd never even met the fellow. To this day I don't even know what he looked like, dark or fair, tall or short. And that's God's own truth. Why do you imagine I should kill a man I hadn't even met?'

Martin said again, 'Lord Kyme has advanced some powerful arguments to my masters. It isn't as if he is simply condemning you without cause, merely on account of some old squabble. He does claim that there is considerable attestation as to the present issue.'

'What the devil does that mean, then? Proof of my guilt? What sort of proof?' The frown returned, and

Robert kicked angrily at a nearby fruit bush that was just coming into leaf.

'There is, for instance, the little matter of your knife being found in the man's chest,' Martin went on. 'How would you answer that?'

'Ah, yes, the knife. I'd lost my knife. I tried to tell the sheriff as much, but Kyme was there with a dozen of his bullies at his back, and he shouted me down.'

'The knife that I saw was quite distinctive.'

'I don't for one moment deny that the knife is mine. But I do deny using it, to kill with, at least. I keep saying that I lost it, but nobody ever listens. We come back to the same old objection. Why on earth should I want to kill a man I'd never even met? Answer me that, if you can, and I'll happily answer anything you put to me. But you can't answer it, for it makes no sense.'

'You're sure you'd never met him? Not even for the first time that same day? You didn't even bump into him quite by chance, when you went to Kyme that afternoon?'

'No,' said Robert, a note of despair in his voice. 'I went to Kyme –'

'What o'clock?'

'I can't remember, late afternoon, four o'clock or somewhat earlier, I should think. We dine around three as a general rule, but that particular day I didn't feel very hungry, so I didn't spend much time at the table, and I left as soon as I'd finished. I planned to arrive in daylight, to – to do what I'd gone to do, and then be back here before it was full dark.'

'And had you lost the knife then? Had you it with you when you set out for Kyme?'

'I think I had it with me then.' Robert's brow furrowed

again, but this time in thought. 'I simply can't remember, but I'm as sure as I can be that I had it then. You know that if you're not actually using your knife for something you take it for granted. I'm almost certain that I'd have missed it when I set off if it wasn't there, if you follow me, but I simply couldn't swear to it.'

'So when did you first realize that you no longer had it with you?'

'I do know that I missed it when I'd got back, and was just about to go to bed. My first thought was to go back and look for it right away, but it was getting dark by then, and I decided to wait until morning. I hoped I'd lost it on the road not far from here, and that I'd find it before some wanderer did, and decided to give it a good home.'

'And did you go to look for it?'

'No. I spent that morning attending one of my father's bitches. She was whelping, and it went badly. I have some skill with dogs, I looked after her. Then, as I was about to give some thought to other matters, up rides my lord sheriff, with Kyme at his back, bold as brass, accusing me of murdering a man I'd never met, and knew nothing about.'

'And that was the first you'd ever heard of Wood, or his death?'

'Yes.'

'You left Kyme before the alarm was given, then?'

'I must have done,' said Robert. 'All was quiet when I left. At least, there was a feast going on, so it was noisy enough, but ordinary noise, feast-day noise, as you might say. Certainly no cries of anger or anguish, no hue and cry, or aught untoward.'

'And you say it was getting dark when you got back? What o'clock was that?'

Robert shrugged. 'Seven?'

'You left at, say, half past three, and got back at seven, then?'

'About that.'

'It's no more than an hour's gentle ride there and back, I know that, for we've just ridden it ourselves. You might stop on the road to speak to a friend, but that should not take up too much of your time. Did you stop anywhere, or talk to anyone?'

'No, beyond passing the time of day with a fellow who has a cottage on the edge of our lands.'

'So, by your own account, that leaves you with a good hour, perhaps two hours, at Kyme, does it not?'

Another shrug. 'I suppose so.'

'What were you doing there for all that time?'

'I spent some considerable time outside, for a start,' said Robert with a sudden conspiratorial grin, for all the world like one naughty schoolboy to another. 'Kyme has no great love for me, nor I for him, though that's beside the point. But I did know that his servants were aware of the quarrel between us, and I strongly suspected that they'd had orders to keep an eye open lest I visit there. I had no desire to be slung into the moat by a couple of Kyme's churls, so I waited outside the gate until it looked safe to go in.'

'Then sneaked to the kitchen?' Martin asked innocently.

Robert looked angry for a moment, then he looked at his shoes. 'I made my way there discreetly, shall we say?'

'But then looked in quite openly?'

'Oh, yes.'

'You'd no fears that the cooks would set about you, then?'

Robert's face cleared, and he laughed aloud. 'I'd been at some pains to make myself agreeable to the servants in the kitchens. Daisy, that's the lady I was there to see, is one of my lord's maids, and a great favourite with everyone at Kyme, so that some of the servants, and the kitchen staff in particular, had something of what you might call a family interest in me. Then there's a nice old dear in the kitchen, Martha, who's related to our own cook, Margaret.'

'Ah, I thought they looked alike.'

'Yes, they're sisters. Not so out of the way in a small place like this, when you think about it. Well, I frequently carried bits of news from one to another of them, and consequently Martha and her friends made much of me whenever I was at Kyme. So I really had nothing to fear once I'd got as far as the kitchen in safety. They've hidden me in there from Lord Kyme's eagle eye more than once before today, if the truth be known. I think it pleased them to think that they were intriguing, if only in that small and very innocent way, against their master.'

'And you saw no-one on your way to the kitchen?'

'On the contrary, I saw a good many people. There was a meal laid on for all my lord's workers, and a few of them were leaving the great hall at about the time that I was making my way in there. But I took care that not many of them should see me.'

'None the less some of them did, I believe?'

Robert nodded. 'Fortunato did. The jester, you'll have met him? I'd no fear of being seen by him, though. In fact, we exchanged a few words, we usually do, we're old friends, Fortunato and I. And a couple of men went past me at one stage, I thought at first they were Kyme's men, come to give me the drubbing I had feared, but I didn't recognize them at all. I think they must have been some of the entertainers, musicians or the like, there are usually lots of strangers at Kyme on May Day, that was partly why I went then, thinking I might escape notice the more easily. Anyway, those two must have thought that I belonged there, for they fell silent and touched their caps as I passed them, and I gave them good day, as heartily as I could. With a feeling of considerable relief, I might add.'

'That was in the courtyard?'

Robert shook his head. 'No, that was in the little tunnel thing, you know, the gateway that leads through the outer wall from the village into the courtyard. The two men were going out just as I'd crossed the bridge over the moat, and was about to enter the yard. I was a bit shaken by meeting them, for I hadn't seen or heard them, and I'd rather flattered myself that I was keeping a sharp look out. So I must confess that I did lurk in the shadows a bit then, and that was when I met Fortunato. Then, just as Fortunato left me, who should I see but Ralph Butler? He spotted me, too, I could see that, for he gave a sort of little jump of recognition, and hared off. I don't get on quite as well with Ralph as I do with Fortunato, to put it mildly. So I took it that he'd run off to inform his master that I was darkening his doorstep.'

'He did,' said Martin. 'And so what did you do when you'd encountered Ralph?'

'Well, when that happened, when Ralph spotted me, I have to say that I was even more unsettled than I had been by meeting the two strangers. I crept even further into the shadows, as far out of the way as I could get. I felt quite sure that Ralph would tell Kyme I was there, and feared the consequences. And yet you say he did tell Kyme?'

Martin nodded.

'Wonder why he didn't have me thrown out?' Robert mused.

'I understand he thought about doing precisely that,' said Martin, 'but that Lady Kyme persuaded him to be merciful, its being May Day. But you were about to tell us what you did then?'

'Yes, of course. Good of Lady Kyme, though, wasn't it? I've no quarrel with her. Nor with my lord, come to that, not as such, not a personal quarrel, that's to say. I'm sure he's a very pleasant fellow, easy to talk to and so forth, if you're not a member of the opposing faction. And even that shouldn't matter, should it, to men of good will? I really don't know what the dispute between his family and mine was all about originally.'

'These old feuds can cause a lot of trouble. But you were saying – ?'

'Yes, what was I saying? Hiding in the shadows, that was it. I saw Ralph, so I hid in the shadows. For some considerable time, I might add, because I was a bit apprehensive, wondering just what would happen. Eventually I decided that it should be safe to move on. I thought perhaps I'd been mistaken and Ralph hadn't seen me after all. So I went round to the kitchen door.'

'Then?'

'Then I saw old Martha, had a word with her.' Robert paused, seeming reluctant to say any more.

'Yes?' Martin prompted.

'Well –' The reluctance to speak was very marked now. Robert scuffed the toes of his modish shoes in the gravel of the path.

'Master Middleham,' Martin said, as severely as he knew how, 'a man is dead, and, as things stand at the moment, you are the most likely suspect. I must ask you to be honest with me.'

Robert sighed. 'I suppose you're right. Well, Daisy, the kitchen maid, you know? It was her I'd gone to see. Well, I asked for her, and she came outside, and we talked. Over by the stables.'

'Lovers' talk?' Martin was embarrassed at having to ask such a question. He knew nothing of the sort of things lovers might say to one another, for of course he had never had any sort of experience of the things lovers might say to one another, and yet he had to pretend he did, to persuade Robert to tell his tale.

The answer, when it came, was an odd one, though. 'Oh, no,' said Robert. 'Nothing of that sort.' He stopped. 'Look here – well, I suppose you'll be told, if you don't know already. Daisy and I –' he stopped again.

'You were lovers, I know that much.'

'Yes. We were, in every sense of the word, and had been for some considerable time. She's a delightful girl, of course. You'll have met her? No? Well, you have a treat in store.' The hesitation in his manner returned. Reluctantly, as it seemed, he went on, 'However, that wasn't really what had taken me there on that parti-cular occasion.' He broke off again, and stared at his shoes.

'Having said this much, it would be silly not to get it all off your chest,' Martin pointed out.

'Yes. But it is a bit embarrassing. Worse to have to tell it out loud to some dusty old Judge, though, I suppose. Well then, if you really must know, I went there that day to tell her that everything was over.'

This abrupt end to the hesitant account shocked Mar-tin. 'Over? You mean that having had your way with the girl, you simply intended to ride off and leave her in the lurch?'

Robert considered this for a moment. 'Yes. More or less. I mean, as far as having had my way with her, and all the rest of it, she was a willing participant. Very willing, I may say. And I'd been generous with her, presents and what have you. I mean, did you, or she, really think there'd be anything more? Be reasonable. She's very nice, and all that, but she's only a kitchen maid.'

'But so she was when you met her at first. It doesn't seem to have put you off at all then, does it?' Martin did not mean it to sound priggish, but it did.

'Ah, well. Yes. But then –'

'Yes?'

'Different circumstances, old lad,' said Robert defensively.

'How do you mean?'

'Well.' Robert frowned once more, and kicked the bush again. 'There is, or, rather, there was, someone else. A young widow. Attractive, and rich, which is more to the point. Her late husband was a wool stapler, very wealthy, rolling in money, to be blunt, and she was his sole heir. And my family, though old and highly regarded, unless you count Kyme's opinion of us, and I don't, is nevertheless not a rich family. In fact, there's this place, which my father has pledged to some money-lender as security for a loan that he probably won't be able to repay. And that's it. All our worldly goods. Nothing else, I'm afraid. See?'

'You envisaged marriage with this lady as being a combination of pleasure and business, then?'

'Exactly.'

'But before you could decently marry this lady, you

needed to end things with Daisy? To avoid complications, shall we say?'

'Just so.'

'Yes, I think I do see, now.' Martin could not help sounding disapproving. 'And how did Daisy take the news?'

Robert winced slightly. 'Badly. She didn't shout or scream, or anything. In a way, I think it would have been better if she had, get it over with. She just started to cry, very quietly. What could I do then? There's no proper way to deal with that, is there? Once they start with that, you've had it. And they know it. She didn't seem to hear anything I said after that, so I got out, fairly quickly.'

'Straight home?'

'Yes.'

'And the other lady? The rich widow? You said "was", I think?'

Robert aimed one last, vicious kick at the bush. 'Her father stepped in, found someone else for her. Didn't want her to marry a man suspected of murder. Can't blame him really. But it is damned awkward. And in any case, that should convince you that I didn't kill Wood. Not only had I nothing to gain, but I've actually lost as a result of his death. Even if – when – your special commissioners clear this matter up and prove me innocent, she's still married to another man.'

'H'mm.' Martin tried to sound sympathetic, but failed.

'And, what's worse, I haven't even got Daisy any more.'

Martin coughed to hide his feelings.

Robert went on, 'Are you satisfied? Or must I still appear at a formal hearing, do you think?'

'Now, that must depend on Sir George and the other commissioners. I'll let them know what you've told me, and then it'll be up to them to decide. I have to tell you that you probably will have to stand up in public and repeat your tale.'

Robert sighed. 'If I must, I must. I have to say that I feel a lot better for talking to you like this, getting it off my chest as it were. Tell me, you've had a look at this matter, is there really no-one else who you think might have done this terrible thing?'

'Obviously I couldn't say, even if we suspected anyone else.'

'No, I suppose not. Will you wait for father?'

'We'd best get back, thank you all the same. One last question, if I may. Was your knife sharp?'

Robert looked puzzled. 'Can't remember. No, when I think about it, I don't think I'd sharpened it recently. Does it matter?'

'I'm not sure what may matter. Thank you for bearing with my questions,' and Martin held out his hand.

Robert shook it, a firm, confident grip. 'I'll get your horses for you. Oh, and there was just one thing – no, it's a bit audacious, really.'

'No, anything I can do to help, I will.'

'Well, in that case, could you possibly put in a word for me with Daisy, if you get the chance?'

'What with the other lady being something in the nature of a letdown, as it were?'

'Absolutely.'

'I can't promise anything,' said Martin, trying to keep his voice level.

'No, I see that. But I'd be very grateful for anything you might be able to do in that direction. It is very awkward.' And Robert took them to the stable, then watched as they found their horses and rode off.

At the first turn in the road they looked back, to see Robert still looking after them. They waved, and he raised a hand.

Clement said, 'Nice old chap, that.'

'Yes. Clement, I know that old man so well.'

'I didn't think you knew him?'

'No, I mean that he's exactly like my own father. I can't see that he'd tolerate anything dishonourable at all. And thus, of course, I can't believe that the son would do anything dishonourable. Not been brought up to do it, you see.'

'Aye, perhaps so. And yet he does seem to have – what's the word? – trifled with this Daisy's affections. Trifled with a damned sight more, too, by what he was saying.' •

Martin waved a hand dismissively, partly because he felt that he had sounded too much like a clergyman when he spoke to Robert, and partly because he remembered certain of his old schoolfellows, men who would have, and in some cases had, behaved exactly like Robert. 'Only to be expected, a healthy young chap like that,' he said. 'Wild oats, and so forth. That's one thing, killing's another. I can believe that Robert might kill in anger, and regret it at once, or that he'd answer in kind if challenged or provoked, yes. But not this skulking in shadows.'

'So we can dismiss him, think you?'

'That's the snag, Clement, we really cannot. You see, this maid, Daisy, stumbled over Wood's body near the stables. Now, she might well have had to go in and out of the kitchen into the courtyard, in the course of her duties, it's true. But none of that would take her anywhere near the stables, which are right over at the other side of the courtyard from the kitchens, and the great hall. Agreed?'

Clement nodded. 'Agreed.'

'So, when Wood was killed, Daisy must have been over near the stables to begin with, or she'd not have seen the body. That's the first thing. The second thing is that she was over there for some reason unconnected with her duties. And Robert said that when he spoke to her, it was over by the stables that they talked. That can only mean that they must have been there at about the time that Wood met his death.'

'And that proves that Robert was not merely at Kyme when Wood was killed, but that he was at almost the self-same place in the courtyard? And at the right time, too?'

Martin nodded without speaking, and kicked his horse into a smarter pace, leaving Clement a good way behind him. Clement thought for a moment; then decided that his master wanted to be by himself, so he made no attempt to catch up.

Five

As they rode through the gate, Martin said, 'We must talk to this girl, Daisy, as soon as possible.'

'Why her?' asked Clement.

'It may be that she can say when Robert left the courtyard to go home. He had just told her that he was deserting her, remember, and she was upset as a consequence. What more natural than that she should look after him as he left her, follow his every move?'

'Most likely had her apron thrown over her head, crying away nineteen to the dozen,' said Clement. 'That's what they do, you know, master. Would she be in any state to notice anything, think you?'

'We can ask, in any event.' Martin turned towards the house, almost bumping into Lord Kyme, who was making for the stables, Fortunato at his back. Kyme nodded to Martin in an off-hand way, but Fortunato bowed deeply.

Emboldened by his successes thus far, Martin said, 'My lord, there was something I meant to ask you.'

'Well?'

'I should like your permission to spend some time talking with some of the servants. To ask whether they noticed anything out of the ordinary at the time of Master Wood's death. Sir George has given his approval of the undertaking,' he added hastily, fearing that Kyme's reply would not be sympathetic.

'I must say I can't see what you hope to find out – after all, if they'd seen anything odd, they'd have told me at the time, wouldn't they? – but, if you think it will help, then by all means ask anything you like, with my blessing. Anything that'll bring this sad business to a successful conclusion is worthwhile.'

'Thank you, my lord. It was one of your lordship's kitchen maids I really wanted to talk to, Daisy by name.'

Kyme nodded. 'Do as you wish.'

'You'll like Daisy,' added Fortunato. 'Nothing crushed about our Daisy, eh, my lord?'

Kyme stared at the dwarf jester. 'What? What d'you mean?'

'Why, Daisy would make any man grow to twice his size.'

Clement guffawed, while Kyme and Martin stood puzzled.

Fortunato bowed to Clement, and said, 'The churl understands what the lord and the clerk do not. Curious, do you not think, my lord?'

Kyme said, 'The churl understands the fool because he's a fool himself. You're a pair of damned fools. Get out of my sight, both of you,' and he strode angrily into the stables, Fortunato bowing gravely after him.

Martin gave Clement a look which wiped the smile off his face, and started towards the house, with the others following him.

'Fortunato,' Martin said as he went, 'you saw young Robert Middleham on the day that Master Wood was killed, I believe?'

Fortunato skipped ahead of Martin, turned and bowed.

'In fact, you spoke to him?'

Another bow, politeness itself on the face of it, but

Fortunato's eyes were shrewd. 'Master Middleham told you that, I take it? For no-one else knew of it.'

'You didn't feel it incumbent upon you to tell your master that the young man was here?'

Fortunato stuck his tongue out, and made a rude noise.

'And yet Ralph, who also saw Robert Middleham, did feel it his duty to tell Lord Kyme of it?'

Another rude noise, louder this time. Martin stood his ground and waited. Fortunato shrugged, and said, 'Ralph obviously thinks that he can win my lord's approval by telling tales out of school. Ralph is – well, Master Clerk, I've no wish to shock you, for you're a nice, innocent young man, and educated by the holy fathers to boot, but I don't mind telling you that I don't have a great deal of time for Master Butler. On the other hand, I do have a great deal of time for Robert Middleham, who, for all that he's a gentleman, always has time for a wave, or a word, even for me.' Fortunato led them inside, marched across the great hall, now almost deserted, and sat in Lord Kyme's chair at the high table. He waved them to seats either side of him.

'What sort of a man was Wood?' asked Martin.

'Wood? He was a merchant. Rich, at least compared to most men. Agreeable enough. Even kindly, in his way.'

'And what way was that?'

'My, my, Master Clerk, what sharp ears you have! Why, a merchant's way, to be sure. An eye to profit and loss. What other way did you think I meant?'

'Did you like him?'

Fortunato put his head on one side, considering the question. 'Yes.'

'Why should anyone want to kill him?'

Fortunato shrugged. 'Why do you think anyone wants to kill anyone?'

'Robbery is the obvious motive, yet his purse was untouched, I understand.'

Fortunato reached out and picked three walnuts from a dish on the table. He cracked them between his fingers, passed one to Martin and one to Clement, and popped the other into his mouth.

'Hate?' Martin went on.

'Perhaps. He may have made more than one man smart in the way of business, for all I know. What merchant does not? But if there's one thing certain it is that he had no enemies of that sort here at Kyme. My lord always made him welcome, and would have liked to see him more often, he's said as much many a time.' Fortunato laughed. 'As did my lady, made him welcome, I mean. And as for the rest of us, we had nothing to do with Wood, his goods were not for such as me, or the other servants.'

'Envy? Jealousy?'

'Envy because he was rich, and killed because of it? Pointless, Master Clerk, pointless.'

'You say that my lady always made Master Wood welcome?' asked Martin – but cautiously, for he sensed that these were dangerous waters.

'Yes, you do have sharp ears. A useful thing, I suppose, for a man who will be a judge himself one day.'

Martin flushed. 'You flatter me. But that doesn't answer my question.'

'Well, then, I meant it only in a most general sense, Master Clerk.' Fortunato put his head on one side, and considered. 'It's true that my lady did seem to have a soft spot for Master Wood. She kept to her room for a couple of days when he was killed, I recall. But I'm certain it was nothing, just ordinary friendliness, hospitality, call it what you will. There was nothing at all – untoward, shall we say? And precious little opportunity for anything of that sort, I might add. Remember, a fine lady is forever surrounded by her maids and attendants, even when husband is away from home. Especially when her husband is away from home.'

'And I suppose the family jester is usually to hand, as well?'

Fortunato laughed. 'Usually. If you're asking the question I suspect you're asking, then, no, I never saw anything out of the way in that direction. There was never the opportunity, as I say.'

Clement shuffled in his chair. 'Aye, but was it only lack of opportunity that prevented anything – untoward, was it you said? After all, it's a known fact that plenty of highborn women have a secret yearning for – what can I call it?'

'A bit of rough?' suggested Fortunato.

'The more homely, down-to-earth sort of man, let us say. I mean, I can tell you –'

Martin cleared his throat ostentatiously.

'Be that as it may,' said Fortunato, 'all I can swear to is that there was never anything of that sort at Kyme.'

Martin asked, 'Do you have any suggestions, then? Any reason why Wood should have been killed?'

'Perhaps someone mistook Wood for another man?'

'Such as?'

'Ralph. I could understand hate being a motive if that were so.'

Martin waved a hand dismissively. 'It was full daylight.'

'It was late afternoon. The sun was low, there were

dark shadows cast by the walls of the house. A man who had been drinking heavily, and most of them had, I know I had, and then coming out into the courtyard, dazzled at first by the sun, then going into the shadows, he might easily mistake Wood for someone of the same height and build.'

'He was similar to Ralph?'

'Aye, Ralph himself said as much.' Martin regarded the dwarf curiously. 'And you think that something of that sort may have happened?'

'Not in the least,' said Fortunato cheerfully. 'I only mention it to show the sort of improbable thing that could – could – have happened. I think the real explanation is something much more simple. So simple, so easy, so obvious, that it escapes notice. Like a wart on the end of your nose,' he added, gazing fixedly at Clement's nose.

Clement crossed his eyes, trying to see the end of his nose. Martin could not restrain himself from clicking his tongue in sheer annoyance.

'I'm not being much help, am I?' Fortunato asked, a specious note of concern in his voice.

'Not much,' Martin agreed. 'I think we'll leave it there for the moment, good Fortunato, with many thanks for your trouble. And now, Clement, I think we'd better talk to Daisy.'

Clement, who had been looking forward to this for some time, rubbed his hands together. 'Follow me, master.' He led the way to the kitchen, and Martin followed. Clement moved easily through the kitchen, smiling and passing the time of day with everyone, until he came to Martha. He asked, 'Is Daisy around just now?'

Martha pointed to the other side of the room. 'Over there.'

Clement waved to Martin to join him, and went across to where a young blonde woman, no more than twenty years old, stood slicing bread.

'Daisy?'

The girl looked up, startled. She was everything that Clement had expected, long blonde hair, a face that a man might die for, generous as to breasts and bottom. Clement sighed. What a waste, stuck here amongst farm labourers and scullions. Still, the call of duty rang loud in his ears. Reluctantly he said, 'Master Byrd here would like to ask you a few questions.'

Martin smiled at her, as reassuringly as he knew how. It did not seem to work, Daisy looked as if she were about to burst into tears.

'Only a very few questions,' Martin told her, 'about young Robert Middleham.'

The tears did come then, lots of them. Clement took Daisy's hand, and patted it, while several of the servants looked across at them, obviously wondering just what might be going on.

'Look here, this place is no use for a private talk,' said Martin. 'Let's go outside for a moment.'

Once outside, Martin found a quiet spot in the courtyard. 'Now, Daisy,' he began, trying to reassure her, 'you know why we're here, I'm sure. Sir George and the other commissioners thought you might feel happier talking quietly to me, instead of having to speak at a formal hearing.'

Daisy certainly did not look happy. Anxious to avoid any further tears if at all possible, Martin hurried on, 'We just want to ask you a few straightforward questions about Robert Middleham, that's all. We know that he came to see you, and why, so I won't go into that. But what I want to ask is this – when Robert left you, you started back to the kitchen, and stumbled over Master Wood's body, is that right?'

'Oh, no, sir, that was later.' And, having managed that, Daisy gave way to the tears that had never been too far away.

Martin started to speak, then realized he would only make matters worse. He looked at Clement, who just shook his head as if to disown all knowledge of the matter, then took Martin's arm and steered him a few paces away from Daisy. 'Master Byrd,' said Clement confidentially, 'the real trouble is that the girl's scared to death of you. Not you as such,' he added, as Martin looked offended, 'but with you being more official and clerical, like. The law on your right shoulder, and the Church on your left, so to speak. Now, if I could just have a word with her, alone, I might be able to get her to tell me something more. How about it?'

Martin was taken aback by this but quickly realized that Clement was probably right. Daisy very probably would be happier talking to Clement, with his big grin and down to earth speech. He nodded. 'See what you can find out.'

Clement grinned happily, went over to Daisy, who was standing in the same place, still crying into her apron, and put a brawny arm round her waist.

Martin, very conscious of not being needed at this juncture, smiled weakly at Clement, then started towards the door to the great hall. It was not more than an hour or so until dinner time, so Sir George and the others ought to be back fairly soon. Sir George was not, Martin knew, a man who took kindly to missing his meals.

He walked over to the main gate, and stared down the road. There was no sign of the others, and Martin, not wanting to loiter around the house on his own without anything specific to do, decided to walk down into the village and look in at the church.

It did not take more than five minutes to reach the church, a substantial stone building. Martin went inside, and spent a few moments in quiet prayer, breaking off when the door opened and a man in clerical garb entered. Martin stood up, and walked over to him.

'Good afternoon, father.'

'Good afternoon, my son. I saw you enter the church, and thought perhaps you wanted to see me.' He looked more closely at Martin. 'Ah, you'll be with the party from London?'

'That's so, father. I found myself with an hour to spare, and it's a while since I was inside my own church.'

The priest nodded approval. 'I'm sorry I disturbed you. I'll leave you alone again.'

Martin caught an odd note in his voice, almost wistful, as if the priest had little in the way of company in that isolated little village, and would be glad of someone to pass the time of day with. He said, 'No, I feel better already for my visit. If you are not too busy, perhaps we could have a short talk? I'm a stranger in these parts, and I'd value your opinions.'

'Not busy in the least. Come along,' and he bowed towards the altar with its great carved wooden crucifix, and led the way outside.

Martin blinked at the daylight after the gloom of the church, irresistibly reminded as he did so of his sojourn in the dungeon. He was now able to take a proper look at the priest, who proved to be a tall middle-aged man with broad shoulders, a man who looked more like a blacksmith than a cleric.

'Father Gerald. Pleased to meet you.' He held out a huge hand.

'Martin Byrd.'

Father Gerald put his head on one side, closed one eye, and squinted at Martin.

'My father has an odd sense of humour. I was born in spring, and there are always lots of martins round the barn at home. And with the family name being Byrd –'

'I see. Very appropriate, in fact. Well, as for that, I used to be a carpenter, and that's quite appropriate as well, for a priest, isn't it? Now, my little house is only a short distance off, down this way,' and Father Gerald set off with enormous strides, setting a pace that came close to making Martin run to keep up.

They came to a little cottage, indistinguishable from the others round about it. 'Here we are. I don't believe that the Church should be remote from those it serves, though I know there are some who would disagree. Come in, come in.'

Father Gerald held the door open for Martin, waved him to a seat, and poured a mug of ale without bothering to ask if he wanted one. 'You're one of the special commissioners, then?'

'Only their secretary.'

'Ah, I see. I thought they'd gone off to Norwich, and I knew I hadn't seen them return.'

'Sir George Maryon – he's the head of the commission – asked me to look into a small matter on his behalf.'

Father Gerald shook his head. 'A bad business. But then again –' and he stopped, and shook his head again.

'Yes?'

'Well – are you a cleric? I take it you are.'

Martin nodded.

'Well, then, I can speak freely to you. I'm not one of your hell-fire and damnation priests, I think the Church should be the servant of its people, not a tyrant set over them. But, that said, I disapprove of the celebration of a pagan festival.'

'Lord Kyme's Maying, you mean?'

Father Gerald nodded. 'I know they say it's a harmless sort of thing, but who can say for certain? All I know is, it was here – in England, I mean – long before the word of God came here, and that means that it is irreligious, as far as I'm concerned.'

'And?'

'And, though it may sound odd to you, I wonder if it wasn't some sort of warning, or judgement. What do you say?'

'It's not a festival the Church recognizes, that's true enough. I was saying as much to my own servant just lately. But, as to the other matter –' Martin hesitated.

'Go on, I shan't be offended.'

'I haven't been involved with the law for so very long, and I haven't been involved in any cure of souls at all, but I have seen enough to be aware that there is plenty of evil in this world without necessarily having to look to the next one for it. The devil has no trouble at all finding men to do his work for him, aye, and do it with a will, too.'

Father Gerald threw back his head and laughed. 'Well said, Master Byrd.' He grew serious again. 'And yet, there seemed no reason – no earthly reason, in the most literal sense – for Master Wood's having been killed like that.'

'It is a puzzle. But I feel sure we ought to be able to throw some light on the matter.'

'Any hint as to where you must look?'

'I fear not, not just at the moment.'

'Here, I'm keeping you gossiping, when you'll be wanting to get back to your dinner.'

'No, not at all.'

'It's the consequence of being stuck in an out of the way place like this, I fear. Makes us all keen for news of the big wide world. And perhaps, though I shouldn't really say this, but perhaps it is worse in the case of a man with some little education, some knowledge of the world outside this village. That's why I hoped I might persuade you to come back here for a chat with me. Anything fresh from London?'

'Very little. Suffolk is still under attack. I take it you'll have heard of that?'

Father Gerald nodded. 'My lord is of Suffolk's party, though he seldom bothers to venture as far as the court himself. He's good enough to invite me to dine at Kyme every so often, and that keeps me up to date a little bit. And now, I really will let you go. Feel free to look in if you'd like a talk, any time.'

Martin thanked him, and set off back towards Kyme. As he left the last of the cottages behind him, he heard the clatter of hooves, and reached the bridge over the moat in time to see Sir George and the others arrive there.

Sir George pulled up his horse as he reached Martin, and nodded an abrupt greeting. He seldom bothered to hide his true feelings, and at the moment he looked extremely angry. Martin felt that he should say something, but Sir George's expression did not encourage polite conversation. It was no use asking if all had gone well, for clearly it had not.

'Ah – did you see my lord sheriff?' he ventured at last.

Sir George laughed, a short barking laugh, not of humour but of contempt. 'My lord sheriff is away, gone on some tax-gatherer's mission. It will be two days before he returns, so we are stuck until then, unable to arrange anything. Still,' he went on, more cheerfully, 'the ride has given us all an excellent appetite, so it has not been completely wasted. And you, Master Byrd, have you anything heartening to tell us?'

'I think I may say that my day's work has been slightly more productive than your own, Sir George.'

'That's something, then. Let us see to our horses, and we'll join you in our chamber in a moment or two.'

Martin went inside. The great hall was bustling with preparations for dinner, which would not be too long now, but Sir George and the others had a private room at their disposal, and it was quiet in there. Martin had only a short while to wait before Sir George and the others came in and sat down.

'Now,' said Sir George, 'your news.'

In a few words, Martin told the others what he had discovered thus far. When he mentioned the fact that Bertram was Wood's heir, the atmosphere changed perceptibly.

'That might explain much,' said Sir George. 'The purse being untouched, that always struck me as odd, you know. And Bertram being found out there. He could easily have shammed surprise, pretended to be upset. Our net begins to close around Master Bertram, don't you think?'

'But then,' Martin felt obliged to say, 'a very clever man in such a case might have thought to take the purse anyway, to make it look as if robbery, by one of the wandering players, shall we say, had been the motive.'

'Oh, I don't see that that's a very telling objection,' said Sir George. 'I don't dispute that it's true enough as far as it goes, but then perhaps Bertram is just not very clever, he just didn't work that out as you did. Or perhaps he intended to do just that, to take the purse, but when he had killed his master, the full horror of the deed made him forget about the purse. That's possible, isn't it?' he asked Timmons and Killane.

Killane nodded. 'Or again, Wood may have made some sound when he died, and the servant's guilty conscience may have made it seem louder than it was, so that he ran away without completing his work. In fact, it seems to me that there are plenty of plausible explanations that would meet all the possible objections. The truly significant point is surely that this Bertram had something to gain, and nobody else at Kyme did, so far as we can tell at this stage.'

'This is all very well,' said Sir George with a frown, 'and it seems as if this Bertram had good reason to kill his master, and he was outside at about the right time. But what of the knife? That's Robert Middleham's, at any rate, proved and admitted. Indeed, it's the only really certain fact in this sorry mess.'

'He does insist that he lost it,' said Martin. 'I am bound to say that I was very favourably impressed by the young man, and very reluctant to believe that he killed Master Wood. He seems so ordinary, so decent.'

'It doesn't always follow,' said Killane. 'I've known a great many plausible rogues, even likeable rogues, in my time. Hanged a good many of them, too. No, what strikes me as more to the point is that this young Middleham does not seem to have had any good reason to kill Wood, whereas this Bertram, by contrast, would appear to have had excellent reason. Whatever the truth of the matter, it's clear to me that we must surely question Master Bertram very closely. Do we know where he lives?'

'No, by Heaven, we don't,' said Sir George. 'He seems to have drifted away from the scene without drawing any attention to himself, which is suspicious to begin with. I wonder if that butler fellow would know where he lives?'

'I'll ask him,' said Martin, and went to the kitchen, where Ralph told him that Bertram had taken over Wood's business in Yarmouth, a score of miles away to the east.

'We'll have to talk to this Bertram,' said Sir George, when Martin returned with this information.

'If he's still there,' said Killane.

'What?'

'He has had a year to make his plans. If I'd killed a man in order to inherit his wealth, I don't think I'd sit around waiting for the authorities to decide that it was me they wanted to hang. Of course, if it were a country estate that I'd inherited, there might be some difficulty, but a town house, easily saleable gems, and the like? I know what I'd do in those circumstances, I'd sell up at the best price I could get, and clear out before anyone had managed to work out the truth.'

'By God, yes. Never thought of that.' Sir George frowned. 'Look here, Martin, you've done remarkably well thus far, a fact that I'll make clear to the Lord Chancellor at the earliest opportunity. You obviously have a flair for this sort of thing. Now, how would you like to continue with the good work? How would you like to go into Yarmouth – half a day's easy ride for you – see if this fellow's still there? If he's not, if he did sell up at once and do a bunk, then I think we can say we've got our man.'

'Not if we can't lay hands on him,' said Timmons.

'You know what I mean. We'd know it was him, then, even if he'd fled. It would simply be a matter of raising the hue and cry, and tracking him down. But the mystery would be cleared up.'

Timmons nodded agreement.

'And what if he is there?' asked Martin.

'H'mm. Ask him if he's prepared to appear before us – no, by God, don't ask him, tell him that he'll be ordered to appear before us.' Sir George gave a broad grin. The others looked at him in silence. He went on, 'See, if he's still there and he did kill Wood, the threat of having to appear might scare him, make him do something silly. Even make a run for it.'

'I can't see what that would achieve,' said Timmons.

'If we were ready for it, if we expect him to make a run for it, then we can arrest him, can't we?' said Sir George. 'I'll tell you what,' he said to Martin, 'draw up a note to the local constable or magistrate, asking for his help in watching Bertram, and I'll sign it. Then we can be sure that the rascal will be taken if he flees. How's that?'

'I think it's an excellent idea, Sir George. I'll draw up an impressive looking document, one that will ensure we get all possible assistance.'

Sir George looked pleased at this. 'Of course,' he went on, 'if he turns nasty, offers you violence or anything, or even if you suspect his answers are not what they should be, then you must arrest him on the spot, and send word to me at once. We'll take him to Norwich, and put him to the question good and proper, the sheriff's men'll soon get the truth out of him then. Take your own man Clement along, of course, just in case of trouble.'

'Very good, Sir George. But if he should answer readily enough, yet say **nothing** of significance?'

'If he seems happy to answer, then sound him out. Ask what he knows of the matter. If he is innocent, then he'll be eager to help, and he may tell you something useful. If he's nothing fresh to add to what we already know, well, it's only a day or so wasted, isn't it? If he's guilty, then your questions may panic him into giving himself away, and then you – or the local constable – can act accordingly. I don't see what we have to lose, and we could solve the whole thing with no effort at all. Right, if there's nothing more, I don't know about you, but I'm ready for my dinner.'

There was no sign of Clement at dinner, which was unusual, and when Martin returned to his room he was somewhat surprised to find Clement already in there, stretched out on the improvised bed.

'Where did you get to? Did you not want any dinner?'

'Master Byrd, there are other things in this world besides food, you know.'

This statement shocked Martin into silence for some considerable time.

'And besides,' Clement went on, 'there'll be some supper laid on before so very long.'

'Ah, that's the Clement I know. I thought you must be ill. Now, to business. Did the maid tell you anything?'

'A great many things.' Clement sat up, a broad grin on his face, and leaned back against the wall. 'You recall that the last thing she told you was that she had stayed outside that afternoon, crying and what have you, while Robert Middleham seemingly crept away.'

'Yes.'

'Well, eventually she pulled herself together and went back to her work. Now –'

'Wait, wait. She went back to the kitchen?'

'So she says.'

'So she did not find Wood's body when Robert had gone?'

'No,' said Clement, 'just as she had started to tell you when you upset her like you did, what with your rough manners and all. But I was getting to that, if you'll hear me out. Now, as I say, Daisy went back to her work, trying her best to forget the earlier unpleasantness with Master Middleham. Then, at some point during the course of the meal, she evidently caught the eye of this Master Wood. He must have been pretty badly smitten with her charms – which you can understand easily enough, any-one would be – because later, as he was going outside to answer a call of nature, he bumped into Daisy, and they got to talking. And, not to put too fine a point on it, they went out to the stables together.'

'Why?'

Clement looked as if he could not believe his ears.

'No, no,' Martin went on, 'I don't mean for what purpose did the two of them go inside there, I mean why did she go with with Wood? And why just then?'

Clement shrugged his shoulders. 'Spite, perhaps? You see, Robert had told her that he'd found someone else, and so perhaps she wanted to prove she could find some-one else? Perhaps it was that. And perhaps some of it was that she was upset, she felt the need of consolation.'

'And wouldn't a pat on the back and a "There, there!" have done just as well?'

'Not with a girl of that sort,' said Clement knowingly. 'There's only one sort of consolation a girl of that sort understands.'

'I'm not sure you're absolutely right about that. Still, I think I can see what you might be trying to say. Upset and angry as she was, she'd be easy enough to persuade. Go on.'

'Well, that's all there is to tell, really. When they had – finished, as it were – Wood set off back to the house, alone, whilst Daisy was adjusting her clothing and so on. She said that she didn't want to be seen going back with him, in case there was talk. You know what people are like, especially the servants in an out of the way place like this. Very understandable. And then, when she did leave, she literally fell over his body.'

Martin could not restrain a whistle of sheer surprise. 'So, that's why she was so upset, was it? No wonder.'

'No wonder, indeed, master. Bad enough for the poor lass to fall over a man's body – any man's body – in any event, but when she'd just lain with the man – well.'

'Well, in very truth.' Martin thought for a moment. 'It could be, then, that if Daisy had left the stable at the same time as Wood did, he might have been alive today?'

'Or Daisy might have been dead as well,' Clement pointed out. 'Had she seen the murderer, her life wouldn't be worth much.'

'I suppose that's true. How long was she alone in the stable, or did she not say?'

'I asked her that. She thinks a few minutes, must have been about five, ten, no more, I should judge. She wasn't certain, and I didn't care to press the matter, in case she became upset again. It couldn't have been too long, though, she was just waiting there until Wood had reached the house – or should have done, had he not met his death in that brutal fashion.'

Martin lit a candle, for the little room was now growing dark, and stared into the flame.

'It does help a bit,' said Clement. 'It means that Wood

must have been killed during the short time – ten minutes, at the very outside – that Daisy was alone in the stable.'

'It means more than that, though,' said Martin. 'It means that where we thought that Robert Middleham had no possible reason for wanting to kill Wood, it now becomes clear that he had.'

Clement looked puzzled. 'How so?'

'Why, jealousy. After all, Wood had just slept with Robert's mistress.'

'Nay, his former mistress, master. Robert had just told the girl that he didn't want to see her ever again.'

'Agreed, but then a jealous man does not always think quite clearly. He might say one thing, and mean another. The fact might be very different from the intention.'

Clement looked sceptical. 'So, we are to picture Robert telling Daisy that he was finished with her, then lurking in the shadows to see if she'd lie with another man?'

Put like that, Martin had to admit that it sounded unlikely, but he tried to salvage something of his theory. 'Young men, especially young men in love, do some strange things. Robert may never have intended to marry this heiress. He may have lied to Daisy, to see what she'd do. Testing her love for him, so to speak.'

'Thin, master, very thin. Skeletal. Robert seemed put out enough at the loss of his heiress, did he not? There was little or no acting there, or I miss my guess.'

'That's true.'

'However,' said Clement with a grin, 'jealousy indeed may have been the cause. Not Master Middleham's jealousy, though.'

'Oh? Whose, then?'

'Why, Ralph's,' and Clement grinned at Martin again, enjoying his evident mystification.

'Ralph? Why him? Had he been Daisy's lover, too, then?'

'So Daisy says. Why should she lie?'

'What, before Robert Middleham, you mean?'

'At the same time, more like.'

'Oh.' Martin was slightly shocked at this. He had no experience of women, apart from his mother and sisters, and consequently he tended to think of all women in terms of his own genteel family.

Clement, who had considerable experience – or at least he claimed as much – shrugged. 'That's the sort of girl she is, master. I did try to tell you,' he said in a confidential tone. 'The very fact that she went off to the stables with Master Wood in that way proves it. I reckon she'd say "yes" to any man who asked her.'

'For shame, Clement.' Martin did not trouble to hide his disgust. 'The poor girl may be a bit foolish, I grant you. Flighty, perhaps. Easily influenced by men who seemed superior to her, rich men. Wood was a merchant, rich, or relatively so, and not a local man, he must have seemed very much above her. And even Ralph, as butler in a great place like this, must seem a very superior being. But that's folly, not vice. Certainly not a reason to say anything like that about the poor girl, slandering her in that disgraceful fashion.'

'Perhaps not, master.' Clement reclined at full length, and stretched luxuriously. 'Still, when I asked her just now, she said "yes" to me.'

Martin shuddered, and covered his eyes with his hands.

Clement sighed. 'Well, that sort of thing makes a man hungry. If you'll excuse me, master, I'll be off and seek my supper.' And he stood up and went out, leaving Martin with his own thoughts.

After an hour or so, Martin decided to try to get to sleep, and stretched himself out on the improvised bed. He had just decently closed his eyes, when an odd noise, a clatter outside the door, made him sit up straight. For a moment there was silence, and Martin was about to lie down again when the door opened, and Clement staggered in. Martin's first thought was that his servant was drunk, not an entirely unknown circumstance, but then he realized that it was more serious. He stood up quickly, and went to Clement's side. 'What's the matter?'

Clement's only answer was a loud groan, and it was then, as he got closer, that Martin saw blood on Clement's face.

Six

'How did this happen?'

'Ouch! Gently, master, if you please.'

Martin finished sponging Clement's head, and said, 'Lucky you've a thick skull. Well, how did it happen? Too much ale, as usual?'

Clement shook his head, winced, began to speak, then seemed to think better of it. He flushed, and looked at the floor.

This was unlike Clement. Martin asked again, 'Well?'

'Somebody set upon me.'

'Attacked you? When?'

'Just now, as I was returning from the kitchen.'

'Did you see who it was?'

Clement looked down again, and mumbled something incoherent.

'What?'

'It was Harry.'

'My lord's constable, you mean?'

Clement nodded, winced again. 'I didn't see him, but it was him. Knocked me over, from behind, then he kicked me as I lay on the ground. I heard him say, "Take that, you –" something or another. It was Harry.'

'I think we'd best see him, get to the bottom of this.'

Martin made as if to stand up, but Clement put out a restraining hand. 'Tomorrow, if you will, Master Byrd.

The gate's locked, Harry can't get out of the place. I need to rest. And it will probably turn out to be some silly misunderstanding after all. Harry's a nice chap, we got on very well the other night.'

Martin thought, and nodded. But he made certain the room door was barred, and sat watching Clement for a long while before settling down to sleep himself.

Next morning, Clement was all for laughing the incident off, but Martin insisted on seeing Harry, and led the way, Clement trailing along behind. Harry's sunburned face flushed as he saw Clement, and his greeting had an insincere sound, to Martin's ear at any rate.

Martin gestured at the colourful bruise on the side of Clement's face. 'Clement was attacked last night,' he said bluntly.

'Oh?' Harry tried to sound surprised, and failed miserably.

'You were recognized,' Martin told him. 'Will you explain matters to us, or would you rather talk to his lordship?'

'No, no. That is, it was me, you're right. I'm sorry, Clement. I'd had a bit too much to drink, that was all.'

'That's scarcely a reason to injure someone who's done you no harm,' Martin pointed out.

Harry looked at the floor. 'Daisy, wasn't it?' He looked at Clement. 'I'd seen the two of you earlier on, you see. Not that I was prying, or anything, but you hadn't bothered to close the door properly, and I chanced to go past. The thing is, sir, I've had my eye on Daisy for some time now. Oh, I know I haven't a hope, and I know about the others, but a man can dream, can't he? So, when I saw Clement here, it hurt me. Then I had too much ale in the evening, and that made me angry, so when I saw poor

Clement here, and nobody else around to see –' and he broke off, and held out his hand.

Clement did not hesitate. 'Think no more about it,' said he, shaking Harry's hand. When Martin raised an eyebrow, Clement told him, 'All a misunderstanding, master, like I said it would be.'

'Very well, if you're satisfied.' As they returned to the hall, Martin could not resist adding, 'See what comes of lechery, though? The wages of sin, Clement.'

Clement shook his head. 'If me and Harry can forgive and forget, you should be able to do the same, master.'

Martin was not by nature hard-hearted. Clement had been with him ever since Martin, having decided that the clerical or monastic life was not for him, had managed to get himself appointed a clerk to the justices. If you were to ask him, Martin could not remember exactly how Clement had come to be his servant, he had just attached himself to Martin, not asking for or expecting any pay in those early days, but content to serve him in the sure knowledge that one day Martin would be a great man, Lord Chancellor perhaps, and then Clement would come into his own.

'You great clod,' he said, trying, and failing, to sound angry. 'Did you really have to do that to the girl?'

'Nothing, master, a mere nothing.'

'I can believe that,' Martin sneered.

Clement looked hurt. 'Well, not nothing exactly. I don't think anyone can point the finger at me. If you'll forgive the expression. No, I meant rather that it was only done to cheer the poor girl up. It did, too,' he added.

'When did you last make a confession?'

Clement studied his shabby boots with some care.

'Doubtless when I last felt I had anything troubling my conscience. Too long, I dare say, now that you come to mention it. You could hear me, master, give me a penance. You have the necessary standing, or whatever it's called.'

'Not I. You'll have to find yourself a priest who's not as generous and forgiving as me. There's a church in the village, and the priest, one Father Gerald, looks as if he wouldn't be too shocked at anything you could admit to. And he'd give you a proper penance, one that would make you think twice about your sins.'

'As soon as this is all cleared up, I promise. Frankly, I thought I'd done quite well last night – I mean, to find out that Ralph had also been Daisy's lover.'

'Yes, I fancy we'll have to have a quiet word or two with Master Butler. Before we set off for Yarmouth, too, for if his answers do not ring true, then our ride may be unnecessary.' Martin paused, and kicked at the dusty ground. 'And of course, there's Harry.'

'Harry?' Clement frowned, puzzled.

'If we suspect Ralph may have been jealous of Wood, then so may Harry. After all, he attacked you from jealousy, did he not?'

'Harry? Oh, no, master, never! As for attacking me, well, that was the beer talking, wasn't it? He'd never have done it sober. Never.'

'It must be considered.'

Clement frowned again. 'Will you tell Sir George aught of this?'

Martin considered this. It was, he knew full well, his duty to tell Sir George of all that he and Clement had managed to discover. It should be Sir George, and not Martin, who asked Ralph, or anyone else, such questions as needed asking. But the plain fact was that the unearthing of previously unknown circumstances had produced a curious sensation in Martin. He felt the excitement of the chase, and he had as little desire to share the kill as any dedicated huntsman who sees the quarry in range.

'I'll tell him that we suspect that Ralph may know something,' he compromised. 'If the commissioners want to talk to him instead of letting us get on with it ourselves, or if they want to be present whilst we question him, then I'll tell all we know. If not, then we'll see him alone.'

'And what of Daisy?'

Martin flushed. 'I don't see any need to blacken the poor girl's reputation by shouting everything from the housetops. She found Wood, and anything else that you may have found out does not alter that fact. It only tells us how she came to be there in the first place. Since that has no bearing on Wood's death – or none that I can see at the moment – I think we'll keep it between the three of us, for the moment. Of course, if it turns out that it did have anything to do with the murder, then that will be different, it will all have to come out.'

They sought out the commissioners. 'Yarmouth today, then?' asked Sir George.

'If you still wish it, Sir George.'

'Of course we do. Rely on you. Now, have you written some sort of screed for the local law officer? Ah, good.'

Martin handed over the document he had drawn up, with some care, yesterday. It was an impressive looking thing, full of 'whereases' and 'undermentioneds', and Sir George grunted with satisfaction as he looked it over. 'Should do the trick all right.' He signed and sealed it, and returned it to Martin, who folded it carefully and put it away. 'Meant to ask if your man got anything from that girl last night,' said Sir George. 'You all right?' he added, as Martin appeared to choke.

'Frog in my throat, Sir George, sorry. Yes, I believe that Clement did – ah – find out something which may have a bearing on the matter. I meant to seek your approval for a few words with Ralph. The girl said something which Ralph may be able to throw some light on.'

'Do you suspect Ralph, then?'

'Not exactly, Sir George. The matter is far from clear. It's not completely out of the question that Robert Middleham may, after all, be involved.'

'Well, I think I can safely say that we all have every confidence in you.' Sir George looked over at Timmons and Killane, received nods by way of confirmation, and went on, 'Keep at it, Martin. Ask anyone you like whatever questions you like, and if any of them quibble about answering, tell them you're acting on my instructions, and with my full backing. Right?' he asked Timmons and Killane, who both nodded. 'That's that, then. And we'll see you again when you've talked to this Bertram – and to Ralph – whenever that may be, later today, or even tomorrow, if needs be. I won't think of going to Norwich again until you've told us whatever you may have learned.'

'Very well, Sir George,' and Martin took his leave, and sought out Clement. He found him outside the kitchen door, talking to Daisy, who seemed not one bit abashed or embarrassed by the events of the previous day, but greeted Martin with a curtsy and a charming smile, causing him to flush, and mumble something unintelligible, before recollecting himself sufficiently to ask if she could tell him where Ralph might be.

'I think he's in the buttery, sir, checking the stores,' she told him.

'Thank you. Come along, Clement,' and Martin led the way through the kitchen. As they went, he asked, 'Was it not in the buttery that we found Ralph last time?'

'Was it?'

'Aye, and checking the stores that time, as well. Is that all he has to do, do you think, or is it a big sort of job?'

Clement smiled. 'It's a cosy sort of job, master, inside out of any rain or wind, and no-one to see what you may or may not be up to. Stool behind the door, eyes closed, that sort of a job. I missed my way, I should have found a big house somewhere, and trained to be a butler.'

Ralph did in fact seem to be rather busier than Clement had suggested, but agreed to answer a few questions.

'What were your feelings towards young Middleham?' Martin began.

Ralph shrugged. 'No feelings one way or the other, beyond a feeling of curiosity as to why he should kill Master Wood. If indeed he did, and I'm not by any means certain that he did, despite my lord's opinion.'

'Did you know why Middleham was here that day?'

Ralph smiled, a sly smile. 'Everyone at Kyme knew that.'

'And it didn't – how shall I put this – it didn't bother you at all?'

'Bother me?' Ralph looked puzzled. 'Why on earth should it bother me?'

Martin coughed to hide his embarrassment.

'Spit it out, Master Clerk,' Ralph told him.

'Well, then. It's a somewhat delicate matter, but I understand that you had – ah – enjoyed Daisy's favours yourself?'

'Oh, I see, that's it, is it? No,' said Ralph, in a tolerant fashion, 'no reason at all why that should bother me. So far as I'm aware, young Middleham is a pleasant enough, well set up young man. No reason for jealousy there. After all, most of the men at Kyme – apart, perhaps, from his lordship, and even then I couldn't swear as to that – have enjoyed Daisy's favours, as you so delicately put it, at one time or another.'

'Really?' The question came from a disappointed Clement.

Ralph looked at him in silence, evidently not deigning to answer a question from a mere servant.

Martin asked, 'Well, is that really so?'

'Well, it may be a slight exaggeration. But only slight. She is, after all, a very – friendly – girl. And yes, I had been friendly, very friendly, with her. But then so had others, including young Middleham. What of it?'

'You see,' said Martin, watching closely to see how Ralph would react, 'since we now know that Daisy had been – er – very friendly with Wood that evening, it may be that the circumstance aroused envy in one of her other lovers.'

Ralph frowned. 'Ah, so that's where all this is leading is it? And I thought it was just a cleric's unwholesome curiosity as to the real world outside the cloister. You think that I killed Master Wood out of – what – jealousy that he'd been tinkering around with Daisy?'

'Not necessarily. But it's something I had to ask.'

Ralph held up a finger. 'Item the first, I didn't know about her and Wood. Item the second –'

'Wait. You didn't know?'

'Not until you told me just a moment ago, no. Daisy hasn't noised it abroad. For obvious reasons, I imagine.

And Wood was scarcely in a position to boast of it, now was he?'

'H'mm. Go on. The second item?'

Ralph held up two fingers. 'The second item. If jealousy of that sort were anything to do with it, then most – not most, then, let's not exaggerate, but certainly a good many – of the men at Kyme would have the selfsame reason to kill Wood. Be reasonable, Master Clerk. If I were not jealous of young Middleham, why should I have been jealous of Wood, even had I known of it, which I didn't anyway?'

Martin exchanged a look with Clement, who glanced quickly away. Ralph went on, 'Now, if there's nothing more? Only I am rather busy. Of course, if you did have any more questions, on behalf of their honours the special commissioners, I shall naturally be only too pleased to answer them.'

'No, there's nothing more, with my thanks to you,' said Martin. 'Come, Clement.'

He led the way across the courtyard to the stables, kicking at the dust in the yard disconsolately. The whole business seemed to get murkier, not clearer. In this introspective mood, he almost bumped into Lord Kyme, who was by the stable door.

'Deep in thought, eh?' Lord Kyme sounded amused rather than angry. 'Sir George tells me you've done quite well,' he went on. 'Brought some new facts to light, and so forth?'

'Facts, aye.' Martin laughed. 'But never a hint of any explanation. I confess, my lord, that the more I find out, the deeper I look into this matter, the more complicated it seems. Hence my abstraction of mind, and consequent rudeness to your lordship, just now.'

'Well, you know my views on this. I won't inflict them on you again, but I must say I've seen and heard nothing that makes me change my mind. Servants obliging, are they? Answering your questions and all that?'

'Yes, with many thanks to your lordship.'

'Well, I'll be off.' Kyme hesitated. 'Look here, anything you need, anything I can – may – do, let me know.'

'There is one thing,' said Martin, emboldened by this change of heart.

'Yes?'

'May I ask a question or two concerning Ralph?'

'Ralph? Why? You don't think he did it, do you? Why, he was in the house all afternoon.'

'No, of course I don't suspect him in that way,' said Martin hastily. 'But I was talking to him just now, and he intrigued me. He seemed a very intelligent sort of man.'

'He is.' There was the slightest hint of envy in Kyme's voice. 'Intelligent, aye. And quite ambitious to boot, but in an odd sort of way.'

'Oh?'

'Oh, there's nothing untoward about it, except insofar as it's always been a bit of a puzzle to me. I mean only to say that he's clever enough to have made his own way in the world, as a merchant or something of that sort. He'd have made a good merchant, been successful, rich. He could have made much more of a fortune than he gets from me, and been his own master into the bargain.'

This was such an unexpectedly human view of things that Martin felt emboldened to ask, 'Why then has he stayed here?'

Kyme laughed. 'I've asked myself that, often enough. There's no sort of family connection, his father was just a labourer, died young, and Ralph came to me as a scullion, and then worked his way up. And that isn't easy, in an old place like this, either. That's why I say he's clever, and hard-working, up to a point. But then perhaps he fears the very thing that some men would value highly, being his own master. Perhaps he thinks he wouldn't be a very good master to work for? Or he may fear that he wouldn't succeed in trade, be fearful of risking his all on a single voyage. And then – by the way, speaking of succeeding in trade, I understand that you're off to see how Bertram's doing, now Wood's left him the business? Let me know how he's getting on, if you will, on your return, for he's a pleasant enough fellow, and if he's running the place as Wood did, he'll have some interesting stock, I imagine. Tell him not to be a stranger at Kyme, would you?'

'I will, my lord. But you were telling me about Ralph,' Martin prompted gently.

'Oh, yes. I was going to say that he may think it's better to be the trusted servant of an influential man than to strike out alone. Lots of men do think that, I'm sure,' he added with a sigh that spoke of personal experience. 'That's what I was talking about when I said just now that Ralph had a strange sort of ambition. Ambition at second hand, so to speak. I must confess that I sometimes find it a bit – odd isn't the right word – creepy, as my old nurse used to say. A little morbid, unhealthy, the way he seeks what I might call reflected glory. Yes, something not very becoming.' He shook his head, perhaps to dismiss the notion, or perhaps because he found it unseemly to discuss Ralph in this fashion. 'I'm certain that Ralph would not be too displeased were I to move to London and take a more active interest in the affairs of the court.'

'But you yourself have no such ambition?' It was out

before Martin could think about it, and he feared what Kyme's reaction might be.

But Kyme only laughed. 'No,' he said, 'Ambition of that sort is all very well for my lord of Suffolk and his like. Make no mistake, that's where the real power lies, and had I ambition of that sort I'd be at court with the best of them. Who knows, I might have been greater than Suffolk. But this life suits me. Quieter, perhaps, less exciting, but safer. For I understand Suffolk himself is now under attack, and who can say just how long he'll be in favour? Or even how long he'll be alive? For, in that line of work, failure is quickly followed by the axe. No, my ambitions are confined to enjoying what I have, and avoiding both the success and the failure of life at court. Now, I know you're anxious to be off and help get this tangled business straightened out, so I won't detain you any further.'

Martin accepted this gentle dismissal with a bow, and set off for the stables, where Clement was waiting with the horses.

They were quickly on the road, the sun bright in their faces, and that greenness which had cheered them both the day before was now even more pronounced. Clement waved a hand round. 'Spring overnight, master,' he announced, lest Martin should have failed to notice it. 'Makes a man's fancy turn to –' and he stopped, unsure that he had picked the right phrase.

Martin only laughed. 'I feel considerably happier myself today, though perhaps for a more praiseworthy cause,' he said. 'The only thing worrying me is this with Harry. It's clear that jealousy can lead to all sorts of unpleasantness. I just hope that nobody else gets hurt. Or worse.'

Clement looked worried by this thought for a while, but cheered up as they approached Yarmouth. The countryside all round seemed to be growing visibly, and the farm labourers, now that the rigours of winter and the enforced self-denial of Lent were behind them, went about their work with a better grace, if not actual cheerfulness.

The first task was to seek out the local magistrate, a Mr Coker. He not only promised to alert the commander of the garrison in Yarmouth, but offered them a bed for the night in return for the news from London. Even here the talk was of Suffolk, and the death of Adam Moleyns, Bishop of Chichester, who had been set on and killed by a gang of sailors in Portsmouth earlier in the year. Although their grievance was ostensibly over money they alleged Moleyns owed them, the murder had brought to a head the public's resentment at Suffolk and what was seen as his misuse of his position.

Martin was a little impatient to be on his way, but was quite easily persuaded that it would be as well to be fresh for the task next morning. Once he accepted that, the evening passed pleasantly enough.

Seven

Martin and Clement rode down the narrow and deeply rutted main street of Yarmouth somewhat later than Martin could have wished next morning.

'Plenty of business done here, eh, master?' said Clement, indicating the condition of the road, which gave evident proof of the amount of heavy traffic, laden carts and the like, which moved through the town.

A passing labourer directed them to Bertram's premises, which were all but on the quay itself, and consisted of a large yard surrounded by a high wooden fence, in which a large gate stood propped open. They rode through this, to see a long wooden shed to their left, and a small house, also wood, to their right. The whole place gave the impression, not of being neglected exactly, but of lacking the close attention it might have reasonably have expected. As they dismounted, the door of the house opened, and a tall, thin man come out into the yard to greet them.

'Master Bertram?' asked Martin.

'Aye. Good day, sirs.' He was in his thirties, as far as Martin could tell, had something of a worried look about him which made him look somewhat older.

'Martin Byrd, sir, at your service. This is my man, Clement.'

'Master Byrd, Master Clement. And what may I do for you?'

'I'm the clerk to their honours the Justices of a special commission,' Martin told him, 'appointed to inquire into the unfortunate death of Master Wood last year.'

He had half hoped that Bertram would look guilty when he heard this, but he was disappointed. Bertram said only, 'Indeed?'

'The commissioners have asked me to talk to you,' Martin went on, 'to see if you might have any information as to the matter.'

'Me?' Bertram shrugged. 'If I'd known anything, I'd have said then and there, would I not?' All at once he seemed to recollect his manners, and said, 'Put your horses over by the shed, and come inside the house, take a mug of ale.'

Clement saw the horses safely attended to – for there was no sign of a stable boy or any other sort of servant about the place – then followed Bertram and Martin into the house, which was plainly Bertram's residence as well as his place of business.

Bertram produced a leather bottle. 'Take a seat. You'll have some ale, I trust?'

'Thank you,' said Martin. He was not particularly thirsty, but it would not do any harm to put Bertram at his ease. Clement, who had been expecting Martin to refuse on behalf of both of them, grinned happily as he took the leather mug from Bertram. 'Your good health, master.'

'And yours, sirs. And now, what was it you wished to ask me?'

'We just want to hear anything you can remember about that sad day.'

Bertram shook his head. 'It's a year, now, almost to the day. The law takes its time, I must say.'

Martin flushed. 'There was an Assizes held late last

year, at which a young man, suspected of the killing, was summoned to appear. He failed to do so, and in consequence of that failure, a special commission was appointed. All that takes time.'

Bertram shook his head again. 'This Robin, or Robert, or whatever his name is, that my lord made all the fuss about? Why should he want to kill Master Wood? They had never met.'

'It would be as well to begin at the beginning, if you would. In that way, we can be certain that you don't omit anything, however trivial it may appear. The matter is very obscure as it stands, and so we cannot tell just what may or may not prove to have a bearing on it.'

'Very well.' Bertram scratched his head. 'I take it you don't want to hear about the early part of the day?'

'Was there anything special about it?'

'Nothing. We rose early, the two carters arrived – they didn't work here on a regular basis, Master Wood hired them by the day whenever we needed them. We loaded up the cart, and we set off.'

'Nothing eventful on the way?'

'Again, nothing.'

'And you arrived at Kyme at what o'clock?'

'Noon, or somewhat before.'

Martin was about to speak, when the sound of a baby crying interrupted his question. Bertram sighed, and started to get up, but a door opened as he did so, and a cheerful looking buxom young woman came into the room and nodded to Bertram, who sat down again. The young woman bobbed a curtsy to Martin and Clement, then went through a second door into an inner room where the baby was, opened her blouse and began to feed it.

She had failed to close the door behind her, and

Clement looked at the proceedings with a good deal of interest, but this incident caused Martin to feel extremely embarrassed. He asked, 'Can we go outside to talk?'

'As you wish.' Bertram took them outside into the yard, and went over to a corner where several wicker crates and baskets stood. 'Sit down and make yourselves comfortable, if you can.'

Martin settled himself on a crate, and asked, 'Now, you reached Kyme just before noon that day? What did you do when you arrived?'

'We saw to the cart, and our horses. Then we spent some little time looking at the jugglers and tumblers and so on, until we could seek an audience with Lord Kyme.'

'Did you know any of the jugglers and what-not? Ever seen any of them before that day?'

Bertram frowned. 'The old blind chap, plays the penny whistle. He's often to be seen here in Yarmouth, when he's not away at fairs and the like. I usually give him a few coppers or a crust, if I have anything to spare. You understand.'

Martin nodded. He asked, 'You didn't notice anything out of the way about him, or any of the others?'

'How do you mean?'

'Did they strike you as acting in a suspicious manner, say? As if they had something to hide, or perhaps were at all affected by Wood's death? Anything.'

'I suppose you could say they were affected by the news of Master Wood's death. They were all scared stiff when it happened.'

'And why?'

'For the simple reason that they knew suspicion would fall on them, as naturally as the leaves fall from the trees in autumn. Who else would get the blame?'

'But they did not get the blame in this case,' Martin pointed out.

'No, but then that was only because my lord Kyme had cast this young man in the part of the murderer. Had that not been so, you may be sure that the local sheriff or constable would have had the tumblers and the rest of them in the deepest, darkest, dungeon in the place, and that for only so long as it took to knock together a gibbet or two.'

'H'mm.' Martin still had less than fond memories of his own sojourn in the dungeon. 'Yes, I suppose that's how it would be. And it's a possibility that the commissioners have already discussed.'

'I should think they have,' said Bertram. 'For why should this young man kill Master Wood? The two of them had never met. No, if it were not for the fact that there was some old enmity between Lord Kyme and the young man, then my lord would have put the musicians and tumblers to the question, and they knew it well enough. That's why they were scared, and that's why they cleared off as soon as they decently could, when it was evident that the young man would be the scapegoat.'

'And so you don't see the young man being guilty?'

'Not he,' said Bertram.

'Then what do you think the truth of the matter is?'

'I've given the matter some thought, as you may readily believe, this past year, and the only explanation that I can think of which makes any sense at all is that it must have been one of those wandering players. Don't ask me which, though.'

'And the reason?'

'Simple. Robbery.'

'Ah, but Master Wood's purse was untouched.'

'Of course not,' said Bertram with some contempt. 'Have you ever known a travelling musician to have any money? It's unheard of. Had the purse been found on one of them, Lord Kyme would have hanged him at once.'

Martin shook his head. 'But that's utter nonsense. Why kill him in the first place, if you were not going to complete the task and rob him?'

'Because they did not think of the consequences until the deed was done. They saw the purse, and their lust for gold blinded them to the simple fact that they dared not be found with it. They killed him fully intending to take his purse. But then, all too late, they realized that they simply could not be found with a large sum of money on them.'

'Well, you certainly have a ready answer for every possible objection.'

Bertram gave a mirthless laugh. 'I've been turning the matter over in my mind for nigh on a year, Master Byrd. I have it all worked out carefully. What I have told you is the only explanation that makes any sort of sense, unsatisfactory though it is.'

'H'mm. But then why could the wandering players not simply take the purse, and flee?'

'On foot? And my lord and his constable, and the men-at-arms, all with fine, fresh, fast horses? Remember, the girl must have given the alarm almost at once. Indeed, she may have disturbed the killers as they started to rob the body. Perhaps that's the real reason why the purse was left. I could believe that. But, had she not done so, then flight would be as good as a public confession of guilt.'

'They could have hidden the money, among their baggage.'

'True, but they must have thought it certain at the outset that their baggage would be searched. They did not know about the young man, or the enmity between him and my lord Kyme – they could not know that – and so they had no means of knowing that suspicion would fall so readily on the young man. And, had they hidden the purse in the courtyard, they'd have been obliged to return to collect it, with all the household looking on suspiciously. No, they killed my master for nothing. They were simply blinded by greed, killed him fully intending to rob him, and then either realized that they dare not, or were disturbed by the girl before they could finish the task.'

'There may be something in that,' Martin agreed. 'Let us return to the events of that day, though. Did you know any of the others who were there?'

Bertram shook his head. 'They were the local gentry. I'd only have known them had they been customers of Master Wood, which none of them were.'

'And neither you nor Master Wood had any sort of talk at all with any of them during the afternoon?'

'Hardly.' Bertram laughed. 'They were on the high table, with my lord and lady, while we were in a more humble situation.'

'Now, when did Master Wood leave the room? Stay, though – did he only leave the once?'

'Yes. He was sitting beside me all the time, so I can swear to that. When the meal was over, not before, he said something as to being obliged to go outside to ease himself, and he left the hall.'

'And did not return?'

Bertram stared at the ground. 'He could hardly return, could he, when he had been killed in that fashion?'

He lifted his head, stared directly at Martin. 'No, Master Byrd, he did not return.'

'And then you went outside as well? When was that?'

'After Master Wood. A good long time after he'd gone out, for I got talking to some churl.' Bertram gave a short, mirthless laugh. 'Talking, indeed! Listening would be nearer the mark, for it was he did all the talking there was to be done. At last, though, I was obliged to interrupt him, and go outside to answer a call of nature in my turn.'

'And it was then you found poor Master Wood?'

Bertram sat in silence for a long moment before he answered. 'I went outside. I was a bit drunk, I know that well enough, but pleasantly so, you follow? I was at peace with all the world. I found a quiet spot, there was nobody else outside at the time, or so it seemed, and I did what I'd gone out to do. Then I was all for returning to the table, when I heard a sound, a woman crying. I went across to see what might be amiss, naturally enough, just as anyone would have done, and then I saw the girl, bending over Master Wood's body. I couldn't believe it at first. I'd been talking to him not ten minutes since, and he was so hearty, so full of life. Not until I saw the knife did I realize the truth of it.'

'Did you know the knife?'

'Not I, though most of the others did, they said it belonged to some young man. How could I know it? I was a stranger in those parts.'

'You'd never been to Kyme before?'

'We'd been there together once or twice, but not recently. Master Wood had not visited Kyme for two years, perhaps three.'

'And the young man whose knife it was, did you see him at all?'

Bertram shook his head. 'I can't tell. They said after-wards that he was not exactly a friend of Lord Kyme's, but had been there that day, so perhaps I may have caught sight of him somewhere about the place, but not known it was him, if you follow me.'

'And the same would hold true for Master Wood?'

'As far as I know. We met only Lord Kyme and his lady. And the Kyme servants, of course. I spoke – listened, rather – to a farm labourer. But Master Wood was with me the whole time, until he left at the end of the meal, and I swear he spoke to no-one I did not know, and that nothing unusual happened whilst I was with him.'

'That seems final.' Martin thought for a moment. 'And after Master Wood was killed, you stayed a few days more at Kyme?'

'I stayed there the next day. There was a great fuss, as you will imagine, with Lord Kyme sending for the sheriff, and then they rode off to talk to this young man who'd come under suspicion. But there was nothing came of that. Even if there had been, would it have brought my master back? And no-one seemed to have any objections to my bringing Master Wood back here for a Christian burial, so I did.'

'I'm sure you did all that he would have wished,' said Martin. 'And you inherited this house, and the business?'

'I did.' Bertram laughed without humour again. 'And I suppose that must be regarded as giving me a good reason to kill Master Wood, in your eyes at least?'

'Nobody is suggesting such a thing. Master Wood had not been ill at all?'

'Not him. Strong as an ox. But why would you ask that? It wasn't illness that killed him, was it?'

'I'm just trying to get a clear picture of him,' said

Martin. Remember that I never met him, I have to rely on the evidence of men like yourself. And he was – what – some fifty years of age, as I understand it?'

'Aye. The prime of his life, as they say. He should have been able to look forward to enjoying his old age, to reaping the benefits of all his exertions.'

'Did he exert himself much in business, then?'

'That he did.' Bertram waved a hand round about him, to indicate the yard and house. 'You can see the state of the place now, but don't for one moment run away with the idea that it's always been like this. When Master Wood was alive, all was neat and clean. Aye, and thriving, to boot. It wasn't just that Master Wood worked tremendously hard, though he did that all right, but he had a special touch, a feel for trade, which I fear I do not possess. Oh, I manage to keep things going, just, but nothing like he did. There's my answer – and my only answer, I fear – to your very natural suspicions of me, Master Secretary. I have the business, but I'd far rather have had Master Wood alive and well and right here this minute. After all, I was to have inherited the business in any event, and Master Wood was never one to throw money away, so if he'd lived, I'd not be any worse off than I am today – indeed, I'd be better off, for the business would be thriving as it used to thrive, instead of being in the sorry state it is in.'

Martin looked round. The yard and buildings certainly were shabby and neglected. 'He was never married at all?'

'No. Not that he was at all averse to the ladies, rather otherwise, in fact. But there was no particular one.'

'Not even a recent one?'

Bertram shook his head. 'No.'

'Would it surprise you to know that he'd had an assignation with Daisy, the girl who found him, that afternoon?'

Bertram stared at him. 'When you say "assignation", what exactly do you mean?'

'An assignation. A tryst, if you will. A meeting.'

'For the purposes of carnal knowledge,' added Clement, with an evident desire to be helpful. 'That means –'

'I know well enough what it means.' Bertram scratched his head. 'A tryst? Had he, indeed?' If it were not news to him, then Bertram was a skilful prevaricator. 'Well, well.'

'So you didn't know?'

'Not I. Though it doesn't really surprise me one little bit. I mean, that girl couldn't have been much more than twenty or so, and Master Wood was no longer a young man, but he could still turn a young girl's head. He was a big man, in every way, vigorous, virile – what can I call it –?'

Clement supplied, 'Full of –' and broke off as Martin's eye caught his. 'Life, I was going to say, master, full of life. What did you think?'

'And you'd no idea?' Martin asked Bertram.

'None. The girl didn't mention the fact, and presumably nobody else at Kyme knew – or at any rate, if they did, they weren't saying. Doubtless Master Wood may have confided in me later, had he not been killed like that.'

'Did he tell you that sort of thing?'

'Well, you know how it is. A little boastful talk now and then, between men. Helps the day along, doesn't it?'

'Had he mentioned anyone apart from Daisy, just prior to the visit to Kyme?'

'No. In truth, he'd been grumbling about lack of

companionship of the distaff sort, just before we went. That's probably why the girl appealed to him.'

'And Wood had not been transacting any business that you were not a party to? Nothing at all out of the way, before his death?'

'I don't really know what you're getting at,' said Bertram, 'but no, there were no mysterious strangers calling at dead of night, no secret meetings. In fact, Master Wood was increasingly leaving much of the day-to-day running of the business to me, against the day when I should take it all over, you see. He himself was always there when I needed advice – which was pretty often, I freely admit it, but he was trying to groom me to take his place.'

Martin looked round the yard again. 'I understand you import rare animals, as did Master Wood in his day?'

'Aye. Curios of all sorts, living and dead. Gemstones, rare animals, as you say, that sort of thing.'

'It's the gems that interested me. Did Master Wood perhaps have any valuables about him, other than his purse?'

'No.'

'You're certain?'

'He'd only have done that, taken any gems or the like, had he a definite customer in mind.'

'What did you know of Master Wood's background, his family?'

'I know he had such a vast fund of out of the way knowledge,' said Bertram. 'Not just as to the goods he sold, for that is something you might expect, but all sorts of things, medicines and herbs, all sorts of things. He must have had a good education somewhere, a good upbringing. I always had a sneaking suspicion that his people had been something a cut above merchants, though I couldn't tell you why I thought that.'

'You don't know where he came from, though?'

'No. He didn't say, and I didn't ask.'

'Never let slip anything as to his family?'

Bertram shook his head. 'I don't believe he had any, not as such. Else why should he leave everything to me, the hired man? If another reason be wanting why I did not kill him, remember he took me in when nobody else would look the same side of the road I was on.'

'So, he decided that you would visit Kyme that particular day,' said Martin. 'You took a monkey and a civet, was it?'

'Aye. And Bella, of course.'

'Bella?' Martin frowned. 'Oh, the dwarf woman? I've met her. But I don't quite follow.'

Bertram sighed loudly, and stared at the ground.

'Oh, I see,' said Martin. 'She was sold to Lord Kyme too? Just like the monkey. Another piece of merchandise.'

'Perhaps it isn't a very dainty trade,' said Bertram, a touch of irritation in his voice, 'but if the fine lords and ladies and kings and queens had no taste for such novelties, then merchants like Master Wood and myself would find no profit in dealing in them. Have you reproved Lord Kyme over his choice of pets?'

'I confess I have not,' said Martin. 'But it's not something that's to every man's taste.' He thought for a moment, then asked, 'And did Fortunato by any chance come from here?'

'He did. Some ten, no fifteen, years back.'

'The name, presumably, was a choice jest?' asked Clement, something of Martin's own distaste for the subject evident in his voice.

'Not really.' Bertram spoke with some annoyance. 'Is he not more fortunate than many a young apprentice lad bound to a harsh master, little more than a slave? Or many a girl forced by hunger to turn whore at the town end? When my folks died of the plague, I was on the King's high road for a half a year. I know where I'd sooner be.'

'Well, every man to his trade,' mumbled Clement.

'At least these poor manikins appeal to the lords and ladies,' Bertram went on bitterly. 'If they were lame, or blind, they would not, nobody would care whether they lived or died. They'd have to play the penny whistle, or hold out their cap for whatever charity might chance to provide, and hope they had enough strength to run away if the constable's men had a skinful of ale and decided to have some fun with them.' He gestured with his thumb towards the house. 'The child in there – you heard it crying? – that's a dwarf child, too, but I'll make damned sure I find a good home for him, he won't starve.'

Martin sat in silence for a time, before asking, 'And you can think of no reason, however unlikely, why Master Wood should be killed in that way?'

'None at all. No enemies, no debts, nobody who stood to gain in any way, however remote, from his death, apart from me, of course. And as God will judge me, I swear that I did not kill him.'

'The commissioners may well ask you to appear before them to say all this once again,' said Martin.

'As they wish. Though I can say nothing to them that I've not said to you. Now, if there's nothing more?'

'I can think of nothing that might be useful.' But there was hesitation in Martin's tone.

'Well? Out with it.'

'Could I take a closer look at the child in there?'

'Why?'

'No good reason. Morbid curiosity, that's all.'

Bertram shrugged to show that it came as little surprise to him, but led the way back into the house readily enough. Somewhat to Clement's disappointment the sturdy young nurse was not to be seen, but the child was in its cradle, and sleeping soundly.

Martin stared at it for a time, then said, 'I'm sure you'll do all you can for this poor little chap. Thank you for answering my questions so readily, Master Bertram. As I told you, it may be that you'll be asked to appear before the commission, so you'd best not stray too far from home for the next few weeks.'

Bertram nodded. 'I'm at your service, any time, sirs.' He led them out again, saw them to their horses, and walked to the gate with them. 'I'd be pleased to think that Master Wood's murderer had been brought to justice,' he said, 'so call on me if you need to.'

'There was just one last point that someone or the other mentioned,' said Martin.

'Ask what you like.'

'It's a somewhat delicate matter.'

'So was Master Wood's death,' said Bertram grimly. 'Ask away, good Master Clerk.'

'Well, then. Someone or the other happened to mention that Lady Kyme seemed to – what can I say? – have a particular welcome for Master Wood.'

'Oh.' Bertram stared at the ground for a moment. 'Well, it's true enough. And it was something that I'd noticed myself, and more than once, if the truth be known. But there's no use asking me what was at the back of it all – if anything – for I haven't the slightest notion.

He was a fine man, as I told you when we were talking about that girl, big and sturdy, with a great red face on him, and I suppose that if I was a lass, I'd have said he was good-looking. I don't know, but I did wonder more than once if perhaps my lady had a secret taste for adventure in that direction.'

'What did I tell you?' Clement asked Martin triumphantly.

Martin ignored him, and asked Bertram, 'And did you get the impression that she had ever indulged any such taste for adventure?'

Bertram laughed. 'No. Or at any rate, not on any of the occasions when I visited Kyme with Master Wood. Or not that I ever noticed. There never seemed to be any opportunity for dalliance of that kind, the place was always full of folk coming and going. But who can ever be absolutely sure about these things?'

'You said you never noticed anything when you went there with Wood. But did he ever visit Kyme on his own, do you know?'

'Oh, yes. Once at least, that I can recall, in the time that I was with him. And I think he must have been there before ever I came to him, because that first time he went there – after I came to work here, that is – he acted as if he knew all about the place. He didn't talk as if he was a stranger, visiting somewhere new for the first time, if you follow me.'

'I see. Not that I think that's of the least significance, but you can never tell. Many thanks for your help.'

'My pleasure. And you will let me know if there's anything more you need to know?' And Bertram stood looking after them as they set out, a hand raised in farewell.

'Where next, master?' asked Clement.

'We'll return to Kyme, see Sir George.'

As they rode along, Martin asked, 'Did you see aught amiss with that baby that Bertram showed us?'

'Ugly little beggar. But nothing wrong with it, at least so far as I could tell. Why?'

'I could see nothing wrong with it either. Yet Bertram said it was a dwarf child,' said Martin. 'How could he tell?'

Clement shrugged. 'It is his trade, poxy though it may be. It's true, they do all look the same at that age, so I couldn't be as sure as Bertram seemed to be. I don't know, perhaps its parents were both dwarves?'

'That could be the answer. We never learned anything about babies under the good fathers, so I don't know the first thing about them, I fear, whether dwarf or otherwise.'

'Nor do I, thank Heaven. Always kept well away from anything associated with them.'

'Oh?'

Clement flushed. 'I trust you'll not be starting all that again, master.'

They reached the first outlying cottages on Kyme's lands late that afternoon. The farm labourers were starting to drift home now, ready for their evening meal, something from a leather bottle, if they were lucky enough to have one, and bed. Martin nodded towards the labourers, and said to Clement, 'I wonder if any of these fellows can confirm what Bertram told us, that he did not leave the house until well after Wood? Perhaps we can find the man to whom Bertram spoke?'

Clement shrugged. 'We know he did not leave right after him.'

'Do we?'

'Well, if he had done so, then Wood and Daisy wouldn't have had time to go to the stables, now would they? Or again, perhaps –'

'Perhaps Master Bertram followed them.'

'Jealousy again, master?'

It was Martin's turn to shrug. 'Who can tell? Or curiosity as to what Wood might be up to? Or maybe Bertram did go out later, as he claims, and saw the two of them, coming out of the stable, quite by chance. Perhaps he overheard some lovers' talk between Wood and Daisy, something to the effect that Wood would never forget her, even that he wanted to marry her? That's the kind of thing a man might say under those circumstances, even if he didn't mean it, isn't it?'

Clement nodded. 'True enough! A man'll say anything at such a time.'

'And Bertram may have taken it literally, thought that marriage was a possibility. Why should it be so odd? Daisy is an attractive girl. And Wood was a desirable catch, rich, well set up. And then he was only fifty, and quite healthy, Bertram himself said that, and Daisy is, what, twenty or so? Had they married, there was a very good chance of Wood's siring an heir. And that might spoil Bertram's chances of inheriting.'

'Indeed it might!' Clement smote his forehead. 'And Bertram could not know that he would make a poor businessman. You have the answer, master!'

'We must try to determine just when Bertram left the house, and these people may be able to help,' said Martin. 'They were all there last year.'

Clement reined in outside a tiny hovel and nodded to the aged couple who regarded him suspiciously from the doorway. 'Were you at the feast last year?' he asked.

'Happen,' answered the husband, while the wife said nothing.

'And did you happen to notice who was sitting next to the merchant, the one who was killed?'

'Jack Miller,' said the man. His wife shot him an angry glance.

'Is there a mill on the estate, then?' asked Martin.

The man laughed, and even his wife managed a sour smile at this. 'There is a mill,' said the man, 'but you'll not find Jack anywhere near it. A bit heavy, is a miller's work, if you take my meaning. No, Jack scratches a living somehow or the other, God alone knows how. He has a cottage over this field, and down the lane,' and he extended a callused finger.

'Thank you kindly,' said Clement.

'Don't tell him who sent you,' said the woman quickly.

Clement tapped the side of his nose and gave her a wink. 'He's a lucky man, is your husband,' he told her.

They crossed the field, and came to a cottage in worse repair than the one they had just left. There was a bench in front of the door, and a short, stout man sat chewing a crust of bread. He stood up as they approached, his eyes calculating.

'Masters?'

'A fine evening,' said Martin, endeavouring to follow Clement's example and put the fellow at his ease.

'Fine enough, I suppose. If you've a horse to ride, so's you don't have to walk miles to get home from your work. And easy work to pass your day, not back-breaking stuff. And decent grub to eat when you do manage to get home, not just a lousy crust.'

'Well, yes, put like that, I suppose it would make a difference.'

Clement did not feel that this was getting them any-where. 'You Jack Miller?'

'What if I am, then?'

'You were at the May Day festivities last year?'

'Happen I was.'

'You sat next to Master Wood, the merchant who was found murdered?'

'Who says I did, then?'

'Everyone on the place,' said Martin.

'They would, the bastards.' Miller threw the remains of the crust away in disgust. 'Well, and what are you going to make of it? Killed in the yard, wasn't he? And I never left the table. Did they all tell you that, as well?'

'No, they didn't,' said Martin. 'So if you want us to know that you had nothing to do with it, it will be as well for you to tell us everything you know.'

'Don't know anything, do I?'

'It's talk to us, or talk to the sheriff,' said Clement.

'Well, then. This merchant was a few places away from me at first, but then one or two of them got up and left, like I say, so he was next to me, you might say, then, but he never spoke, the stuck-up swine. Too good to speak to me, I expect. Well, he's not now, is he? Then he went out, for a piss I suppose, so I was left next to his man, and he insisted on talking all right.' He gave a short laugh. 'Boring sod went on and on, I couldn't have got a word in edgewise if I'd wanted to. Talked a right load of old rubbish as well, he did. Well, after a time, and a bloody long time too, even he ran out of words, and had to go out as well, I suppose for the same reason his stuck-up master had had to. Then there was all the fuss and palaver.'

'The maid, Daisy, came in to say she'd found Wood's body?'

'That's right. The maid. Bit of all right that, isn't it? Not that the likes of us would ever get a crack at it, eh?'

'Oh, I don't know,' said Clement.

Martin said, 'But the maid came in almost as soon as Bertram, the manservant, had gone out, is that right?'

Miller scratched his matted hair. 'It wasn't too long after he'd gone out,' he agreed at last.

'How long isn't too long?'

'Well. Hard to say, isn't it? Almost as soon as he'd gone out, I should say. More or less.'

'Thank you, you've been most helpful.'

'Oh, glad to help. Any time. Always glad of someone to talk to,' and he stood by the ramshackle door and watched as they rode off in the direction of Kyme.

Eight

'What a foul-mouthed churl that was,' said Clement with some disgust, as they approached the house. 'Still, his story does agree with what Bertram told us.'

'It does as far as it goes. And yet I don't know that it proves anything one way or the other, apart from the fact that Bertram had not been outside for very long before the maid found Wood's body. Bertram could still have had sufficient time to kill Wood. How long does it take a man to deliver one blow of a knife?'

'He'd have had to find Wood, though.'

'True enough,' said Martin.

'And he'd have had to find the knife.'

'He may have found it earlier that day.'

'But Wood was with him all day,' Clement pointed out.

'What of that? Wood may have been with him when he found it, we don't know that he wasn't. Or Bertram may have lied when he said he was with Wood all day. Wood is in no position now to contradict whatever Bertram may choose to say. It's a pity Bertram wasn't seen outside, for that might clear him of suspicion.'

'Yes. But he wasn't. If there had been anyone else out there, they'd have heard Daisy's cries, and gone to help, just as Bertram did.'

'True again,' said Martin. 'See to the horses, will you, and I'll find Sir George.'

'Yes, and see if dinner's quite over, would you, master?'

Dinner was over, just, when Martin entered the great hall. Lord and Lady Kyme had left the room, and Sir George, Timmons and Killane were sitting round a little table and playing cards by way of relaxation. They stopped when they saw Martin.

'Had a good journey?' asked Sir George.

'Thank you, yes.'

'And a successful one? What does this Bertram have to say for himself?'

Martin told his tale, and when he had done, Killane asked, 'So the business that Bertram inherited is not exactly prospering under his direction?'

'It certainly does not appear to be,' said Martin, 'and Bertram himself makes no secret of the fact that he is nothing like as good a merchant as Wood was.'

'And yet he could not possibly have known that before he was landed with the job of running the firm,' said Sir George, echoing Clement's remark. 'He may have thought that he was quite capable of making a go of it without Wood.'

'That was definitely not the impression that I got,' said Martin. 'I think that Bertram was well enough aware of his limitations before ever Wood met his death.' He shrugged. 'I may have been mistaken, of course.'

'And you found out nothing more?'

'We talked to a labourer on the estate here who remembers sitting next to Bertram, for the latter part of the meal at least. He agrees with Bertram as to when Bertram left the table, which was a very short time before Daisy came in to let everyone know that Wood had been killed. But I don't see that the fact proves Bertram's innocence, for he would still have had time – just – to kill his master.'

'And the knife?' asked Timmons. 'When and where did Bertram manage to acquire that?'

'That I don't know. But unless Robert Middleham did in fact use his own knife to kill Wood, then the knife remains a difficulty that must be explained in any event, whoever the murderer may have been. Bertram could have found the knife in the courtyard, where Robert had lost it, just as well as any other man could.'

'Yes –' but Timmons broke off as Lord Kyme entered the room.

'I hoped to find you still here,' said Kyme. 'I wanted a word with you.' He stopped, as if not knowing what to say next.

'Yes?' asked Sir George in a mild voice.

'Well, it's the twenty-ninth of April today, you see.'

Sir George and the others looked as puzzled as Martin felt.

Kyme sighed. 'The thing is, I've just had word from Ralph that some of the singers and tumblers and what have you are here, in the village. They're wondering if I plan to have the usual May Day celebrations, apparently.'

'And are you?' asked Sir George.

Kyme looked embarrassed at the direct question. 'To be honest, I wouldn't mind; we've kept May Day here at Kyme for as long as I can remember. But it's all a question of how it might look. A bit unfeeling, as it were.'

'Yes, I quite understand.' Sir George looked round at the others. 'Well?'

There was a silence. Martin ventured, 'If I may, Sir George?'

'Yes, Martin?'

'It might in fact be extremely useful if these wandering players did come to the house. We could perhaps then take the opportunity to speak to them to ask if they can recall anything out of the ordinary last year. Perhaps even keep a discreet watch on them, see if they behave in any way suspiciously.'

'By Heaven, yes! That's an excellent notion. Would that meet with your approval, my lord?'

'It would,' said Kyme, nodding his head gravely. 'Though, once again, I strongly suspect that if any of them had seen or heard anything untoward last year, they'd have said as much then and there, in the hope of some reward. And moreover, if any of them had actually had a hand in poor Wood's death, then they'd hardly be likely to return to Kyme, would they?'

'But that in itself might be useful,' said Timmons. 'If you, or the servants, or any of the musicians who do turn up here can recollect any who might have been here last year, but are not here this, then that might be a pointer as to their guilt.'

Kyme nodded again. 'That is so. And I suppose that if they all return, that would at least show they have little to hide.' He smiled at them, seemingly cheered by the thought of being able to celebrate May Day and at the same time help with the investigation into Wood's death. He went out, saying that he would tell Ralph to pass the word on that the entertainers should come to Kyme next day.

Sir George said, 'Well, Martin, with these players and the like coming back to Kyme – and that was an excellent notion of yours, to bring them here for questioning – then if we do learn anything worthwhile from them, we may well be able to advance this matter quite considerably in the next day or so. The plain fact is, I'm disinclined to ask the sheriff – even if we could ever find the fellow at home when we call on him, which is hellish difficult – I'm disinclined to ask him to set up all the rigmarole of a formal hearing, when we don't actually have anyone in particular in mind to stand in the dock.'

Martin was wondering if Sir George was expecting some reply, when Killane cleared his throat delicately. Sir George looked a question at him. Killane said, 'Would it not be an idea to set up the hearing in any event, summon all the relevant witnesses, and see what comes out under oath?'

'It would take time to question them all,' said Sir George doubtfully, 'and if they've lied to Martin, I can't see why they'd tell the truth to us, even under oath.'

'So you feel there's little guarantee of success?' asked Killane.

'Well, I did not wish to put it so bluntly, but that is my opinion.'

'Oh, and I share it,' said Killane, 'share it completely, but at least it would be action of a sort. I own I am concerned by the fact that we do not appear to be advancing in this matter to the slightest degree.'

'Oh, come now, we aren't doing so badly,' said Sir George. 'We have had testimony from Middleham, from Bertram, and in a day or so we'll have it from these wandering minstrels. We may then be able to piece together the events of last year, and arrive at some conclusion. If we can't –' he frowned – 'if we can't, then we'll do as you suggest and set the hearing up anyway, see what happens there. What say you?' he asked of Timmons.

'I am for waiting a while, sirs. If the matter had been as between man and man, a land boundary dispute, let us say, then I'd be all for having the parties appear, call their witnesses to tell us their tales, and thrash it out in open court. But this mysterious business needs some detailed questioning, some subtle handling, and that is far more likely to bring results if it's done quietly and privily, just as the good Martin has been doing it thus far.'

Martin flushed at the praise, while Sir George and Killane nodded their agreement with it. The conversation turned to who might or might not have had a motive for killing Wood. Martin, not wanting to tread the old familiar ground yet again, rose, bowed, and left, more or less unnoticed. He sought out Clement, and found him seated in the kitchen, eating a hunk of bread and swapping dirty stories with one of the serving men. As Martin entered, the serving man remembered a pressing errand elsewhere, and took his farewell.

Clement waved the hunk of bread at Martin by way of greeting. 'Dinner finished, is it?'

'I fear so. Still, not long to supper time, now.'

'No, that's true. I hear those tumblers and what-not are in the district, and will be coming here tomorrow,' said Clement cheerfully. 'I quite like these old customs.'

'Yes, very nice. Listen, Clement, we are going to have to speak to as many of these musicians and tumblers as we possibly can, to ask if they remember anything of last year. There seems little likelihood that they had aught to do with Wood's death as such, but they may have seen or heard something.'

Clement nodded.

'We may jog someone's memory.'

'Or waste our time?' asked Clement.

'With such a crowd, we would have to be very unlucky if no-one could recall anything. There was another thing.' He stopped, still embarrassed.

'Yes, master?'

'Could you talk to Daisy once again?'

'Easily.' Clement threw away the remains of the crust, and rubbed his hands together.

'Nothing of that sort, if you can help it,' said Martin hastily. 'This could be very important.'

'Yes, master. Of course, master. Anything you say, master.'

'Just ask her if Wood had mentioned anything as to seeing her again. If he'd mentioned taking her away from Kyme, marrying her, anything of that sort.'

Clement shook his head. 'Shouldn't think so, master. Why would he do that? I mean, he'd had what he wanted without any of that sort of nonsense, hadn't he? Still, if that's what you wish, I'll be sure to ask her. In fact, if the matter's pressing, I'd best do it now, lest I forget all about it.' He grinned happily at Martin, got up, and left the kitchen.

Something had been bothering Martin, but he had so far not been able to work out what it was. But now, as he made his way through the kitchen after Clement, and caught sight of Martha as he went, he realized what it had been.

'Martha, could you spare a moment?'

Martha glanced round the kitchen. 'Aye, sir.'

'Let's find a quiet corner. Ah, that will do.' Martin went over to a spot by the door, Martha following him. 'The last time I was in here, you said that Daisy was like a daughter to you, I seem to recall?'

'That's true, sir. So she is.'

'And does everyone here think the same?'

'I'm sure they would do, sir.'

Martin looked long and hard at her, and she lowered her gaze under his stare. 'The thing is, and I don't wish to cast any sort of a slur on the girl, but I hear a somewhat different tale.'

Martha made no reply to this.

'In fact, I hear that some of the men here regarded Daisy in a very different light.'

Martha looked defiantly at him. 'Well, sir, there are those who have nothing better to do than slander a decent girl. I don't say that Daisy isn't what you might call a friendly sort of girl, because she is. A very friendly, loving sort of a girl. But what of that? It takes two to – you know.'

Martin flushed. 'Quite so. But – I don't quite know how to put this – how many of the men at Kyme had she been friendly with?'

'Oh, not many, sir. Ralph, I think. And one of the men-at-arms.'

'Harry, that would be?'

Martha nodded. 'Not that I'm one to gossip, of course. I'd never have mentioned it, if you hadn't asked.' She sighed deeply. 'A bit sad, it is, really. For I think Harry was truly fond of her. Still, she had other ideas, so that's all there is to it.'

'And is Harry a jealous sort of fellow, would you say?'

Martha thought this over. 'No, sir, I wouldn't say that. A nice enough young chap. Like Daisy, he's a friendly sort, if you understand me. A bit simple, really. If you follow me. But not jealous, no.'

'And the other men here, the cooks and what have you. They regard Daisy as a daughter, do they?'

'I'm sure that's exactly what they do, sir.' Martha's tone was defiant.

'And how would they react to knowing that she'd been to the stables with Master Wood?'

Martha stared at the floor.

'Come, now, Martha. After all, you knew that she'd done that, didn't you? Why should others not know it?'

'I didn't know, sir.'

'Oh?'

'Not at first, sir, no. Not until all the fuss happened with Master Wood, and then of course we all started talking about it amongst ourselves, and naturally I asked Daisy what she thought, and then it all came out, about Master Robert saying he wanted nothing to do with her and that, I mean. And she said that her and Master Wood had – well, you know. But I didn't know before then, I swear it.'

'And do you think anyone else knew?'

'Lord, sir, I wouldn't know that. How could I know?'

'Well, then, suppose that one of the older men here, one of those who really did think of Daisy as a daughter, had seen her and Wood go into the stable together that day. How do you think he'd feel about that?'

Martha looked at the floor again, longer this time. 'I'm sure I couldn't say, sir. Really I couldn't.'

'No, I see that. Well, thank you, Martha.'

Martin went outside into the courtyard. He did not relish the thought of joining Sir George and the others in yet another recital of how little sense they could make of the various facts they had thus far learned, so after a moment's standing undecided as to what to do until supper, he went down into the village, and sought out Father Gerald, who was sitting on a bench outside his cottage.

'Good of you to look in on me,' said the priest. 'Anything to tell me?'

'As regards Master Wood's death, you mean? Nothing, I'm afraid. It all looks as murky as ever.'

'I thought I saw some of those same wandering minstrels turning up at Kyme?' asked Father Gerald.

'That's so. Lord Kyme seemed keen to have them, to keep May Day as is his custom. And I must confess that I encouraged him in the idea of inviting them here.'

'Oh?'

'For the best of reasons,' said Martin hastily. 'I thought that, if they were all together at the house, we could more easily speak to them regarding what they might have seen last year.'

Father Gerald laughed. 'I wish you luck with that. I suspect you'll find them none too eager to answer even the simplest questions. Indeed, I'm a bit surprised that they've turned up here at all, after the fuss there was last year. But then, I don't imagine they know that you and the other commissioners are here. That'll come as a pleasant surprise for them.'

'You won't be attending the festivities?'

Father Gerald shook his head. 'No. It would look as if I approved, and I don't. Not that my lord is bothered by my opinion, of course. But, what I can do, I feel I should do, and I can show what I think by staying away.'

'You never think of asking your bishop what he thinks of it all?'

'I never have. We – the Church, I mean – have always tried to let the people keep their old pagan festivals as far as possible. Christmas and Easter, of course. Whitsuntide probably falls closest to the old May celebrations, but not quite. I expect the old ways will die out eventually, but in isolated spots like this, they hang on.' He shrugged. 'Not much I can do about it all. I wouldn't like to wager as to the outcome between Church and State, if it came to it. Oh, the King is a good enough Christian, as is Lord

Kyme for the matter of that, but that's only as long as the Church says what the King wants to hear. If it came down to a question of doing that which they declined to do, would men like Kyme, or Suffolk, or the King, meekly obey a simple parish priest – or for that matter even a baker's dozen of bishops? Frankly, I think not.'

Martin had seen enough of life on the fringes of the court to be able to agree, to some extent at least, with this opinion. It was getting on towards supper time now, and he declined Father Gerald's offer to stay and eat with him, knowing full well that a priest in a small place like this probably did not have too much to spare.

He got back to Kyme in time for supper, and as they ate, Lord Kyme told them that some of the tumblers had already arrived. Martin was eager to start questioning them as soon as he could, but when he went out after supper to look for them, they were nowhere to be found. He assumed that they had found a quiet corner somewhere, in the stables perhaps, and were asleep. He would have liked to seize the opportunity to speak to them, but tomorrow would have to be soon enough, and so he sought his own bed, feeling that he had not really wasted too much of the day.

He had not seen Clement since his return from the talk with Father Gerald, and wondered if he would have anything to tell when he did see him. But Clement was not in the room when Martin sought his bed, and had not returned by the time Martin went off to sleep.

More of the musicians and tumblers arrived next morning, and Martin once again tried to speak with them, but they claimed to be too busy tuning their fiddles, or practising their juggling, to answer his questions. He could not tell whether this was the truth, or whether they simply wanted to avoid speaking to him, though he rather suspected that the latter explanation was correct.

For once Clement too was busy. He had risen before Martin awoke, or perhaps he had never been to bed, and Martin saw him only fleetingly thereafter. Clement bustled about, helping to set up the Maypole in the centre of the village green. He complained loudly that he had been pressed into the job, but he seemed happy enough, when he thought Martin could not see him.

At length Martin grew annoyed. He was annoyed that he could not get on with his work. He had been looking forward to asking questions, to advancing the investigation into Wood's death, for the thrill of the chase was in his blood, and he felt frustrated that he did not have a clear view of the quarry.

He was annoyed as well at the fact that he seemed to be the only one who was concerned with something other than the preparations for the festivities, for Sir George and the others showed no inclination to insist that the musicians should answer any questions – indeed, they showed no inclination to do anything other than watch the Maypole being set up, or take a leisurely ride round the fields and woods of Kyme.

Finally, Martin grew annoyed with himself for being such a churl. It was a lovely spring day, the sun shone down on him, so why was he moping around like this? There was nothing he could do, so he set off for a long ride, heading, whether by accident or design, in the opposite direction to that taken by Sir George.

He got back to Kyme just before dinner, feeling considerably more cheerful than when he had set out. After the meal, he ran Clement to earth, and asked what news he might have.

'I spoke to Daisy,' Clement told him, 'and she says what I told you she'd say, that Wood had never said anything about marriage, or aught of the kind. It was exactly as I said at the first, Daisy was upset after the young man had told her they were finished, and wanted some consolation. Nothing more to it than that, just as I thought from the first. She didn't really like talking about it, she got a bit upset when I asked her today. She gets upset easily, you see. Fortunately, it's quite easy to console her.'

'And what of the musicians?' asked Martin quickly, before Clement could elaborate on this. 'Did you get any chance to speak to any of them?'

'I passed the time of day with one or two of them, nothing more. They were busy with their preparations, you see.'

'But they'll hardly be busy now. Where are they, do you know?'

'The stables, as far as I know. But –'

'Come on.' And Martin led the way out to the court-yard, Clement following with a look of resignation on his face.

They found the musicians in the stable, finishing off their evening meal, apparently indifferent to the smells of straw and less pleasant substances, and to the horses which snorted and jostled at the very shoulders of the diners.

Martin thought he could see one or two suspicious glances as he went inside, and the hubbub of conversation faded. Then Clement walked in, and called out a cheery greeting to one and all, which helped matters a bit.

Martin looked round the stable, which seemed

crowded to overflowing, men, women and children sharing space with the animals. 'Were you all here last year?' he asked.

There was a perceptible silence. Clement said, 'Come, now. Master Byrd and the other gentlemen are trying to clear up this business of Master Wood's death. Maybe some of you can remember seeing something that would help? I know you don't want to get involved with the law – who does? But if you've nothing to hide, then you've nothing to fear either.'

Martin added, 'If any of you did happen to know anything that could help, I'm sure Lord Kyme would not be found ungenerous. He's anxious to bring Master Wood's murderer to justice.'

One of the nearest men said, 'I'm sure that none of us, or any of the others, had anything to do with Master Wood's death.'

'I'm sure you didn't,' said Martin quickly. 'But – what others do you mean?'

The man glanced round. 'Oh, there were a couple of people here last year who aren't here this, that's all I meant.'

'Indeed?'

'The juggler, what's his name?' he called to another man.

'Dickon, you mean?'

'Aye, Dickon. And the fellow with the dancing bear, he's not here now.'

One of the young boys said, 'And the blind man's not here, the one who plays the whistle.'

'Would a blind man be able to stab a big man like that merchant was?' asked the first man. The boy looked abashed.

'Nay,' said Martin, 'anything you can tell us may be of use, however small it may seem.'

'But, a blind man!'

Clement leaned towards the speaker and said, 'See here. Suppose the blind man didn't do it, but overheard some talk, something that would enable him to point the finger at whoever did do it?'

'Suppose he did?' The tone was questioning, not belligerent.

'What if he's been killed to keep him from speaking as to what he knows?'

'He was alive at Easter,' said someone at the back, 'for he was playing his whistle in Lincoln high street.'

There was a laugh at this.

'Well,' said Clement grinning, 'I only said, suppose, didn't I? But you can see the sort of thing that might have happened, somebody seeing or hearing something, perhaps even something that seemed unimportant at the time, but looks odd now. Well?' He looked round.

A silence greeted this suggestion. One or two heads were shaken, but it seemed clear that none of them intended to reply. There seemed no point pursuing the matter, so Martin bade them all good night, and started back to the house. 'How did it strike you?' he asked Clement.

Clement shrugged. 'Folk like that, they wouldn't tell anything, even if they knew all about it, despite what that fellow said about wanting to help. They avoid the law as if it were the plague. Probably a very sensible course to take, too.'

'That's all very well, but do you imagine they do know anything?'

'Probably not. They were probably telling you the

truth. They would be busy with whatever they were doing on the day, and they probably don't mix with the servants here to the extent that they know who's who.'

'A lot of probablys. Well, you're probably right,' said Martin. 'All we can do now is to keep a careful eye on things tomorrow. If things are the same this year as they were last – apart from someone getting killed, of course – then we may be able to get a better idea of just what did happen.'

'I'll keep an eye open,' Clement promised.

'You can keep both open. And that means not drinking too much ale.'

Clement knew there was no use arguing.

Nine

May Day dawned, and Martin woke at his usual hour, feeling considerably more cheerful than for some time past. He looked about him, and was astonished to find Clement already up, standing by the door and grumbling under his breath.

'Nightmare, was it?' asked Martin solicitously. 'Or just fleas?'

'I'm troubled in spirit, master.'

'Ah, the memory of old misdeeds. A clear conscience is worth a lot.'

'This is no laughing matter,' said Clement, and indeed he looked very unlike his usual self.

'Sit down, for Heaven's sake,' Martin told him, 'and tell me what it is that troubles you.'

'The day, for one thing,' said Clement. 'Not pleasant May weather at all, is it?' He gestured at the little window, which showed a dull, overcast sky.

'Is that all?'

'No, master, not by any means, but this miserable morning did set me off wondering as to the rightness of what we hope to do. This business of carrying on with the May festivities as if nothing were amiss, I mean. Almost as if Master Wood had never been killed like he was. Or as if it didn't matter that he had been. It all seems very heartless to me.'

'But we are doing it for a good reason, after all,' Martin pointed out. 'We hope to find who it was killed Master Wood. So it isn't only a celebration, but rather a part of our whole task. Don't you think that makes a difference, gives the whole thing some purpose?'

Clement looked unconvinced. 'I take your point, master. But, even so, does it not strike you that we're tempting fate, almost? Almost that we were hoping that whoever killed Master Wood –' and he stopped and shrugged his shoulders.

'You're thinking that he might be likely to do it again, you mean? Kill someone else?' Martin was about to say more, to scoff at the idea, but the look on Clement's face prevented his doing so. Instead he asked, 'You're really bothered by this, aren't you?'

'I own I am, master. I'm not a particularly religious man, nor even superstitious – no more than another – but this strikes me as being all wrong. Almost blasphemous.'

Trying to make him feel better, Martin said, 'The local priest, Father Gerald, had similar misgivings about the May Day festivities. He thinks they're unholy, a relic of the old pagan religion.'

'Does he indeed?'

Martin detected an odd note in Clement's voice. 'Well?'

'Just wondering,' Clement mumbled.

'As to what, exactly?'

'Well, you know. Just whether this Father – Gerald? Whether he disapproves not only of May Day, but of those who keep May Day. Strongly disapproves, I mean.'

'I don't follow you, I'm afraid. Oh! You don't think Father Gerald had anything to do with it? Some sort of religious madness, causing him to wreak vengeance on the sinners? I hardly think so. He doesn't usually attend the festivities, so he'd stick out like a sore thumb had he turned up here that day. Mind you,' he added thought-fully, 'I can picture him being quite – not pleased, ex-actly, that's the wrong word – but what I might call vindicated by what happened. As if it had been a judge-ment, so to speak.'

'And do you think it was?'

'Not me,' said Martin. 'I think it was some evil man. The question is, which evil man?'

'Well, I'm not so sure,' said Clement, evidently unwill-ing to be cheered up so easily. 'After all, if the local priest has these qualms about the festivities, who am I to argue? It needn't have been him, when you think about it – it could be those old pagans, or their gods, come to claim their own. And what are those old gods but the Evil One himself?' and he crossed himself at the prospect.

'If Satan had aught to do with the matter, it was at second hand, and he was working through the agency of one of his creatures.'

'That may not be as funny as you seem to think,' Clement told him with a serious face.

'What, some witch, or wizard, performing some weird sacrifice to his master?' But Martin's tone was not quite so bantering now.

Clement shrugged. 'What's that thing you were talking about just lately? Something about combing witches, though it really means burning them?'

Martin frowned at him. 'Oh, "De Haeretico Com-burendo", you mean. Ah, well.' And he shrugged, unable to find a cogent argument. If it made sense for the Pope to legalize the burning of heretics and those accused of witchcraft, why could those who would qualify for the flames not try to get their own back occasionally? 'Still,' said he, 'though you may – may – have a point there, I'm not going to let your morbid mood spoil the day for me. Come on, let's get some breakfast, that should make you feel better.'

'I can't say as I'm hungry, to be honest.' And it was with a lack of enthusiasm most unusual for him that Clement trailed to the kitchen at Martin's back. Still, once seated at the table, his appetite seemed to return quite marvellously, and he ate more heartily than was usual even for him, giving a sheepish grin when Martin raised an eyebrow, and ventured to remark as to this miraculous recovery.

When they emerged into the courtyard, the day had brightened up, and the sun was trying to break through the thin clouds. Clement stretched, yawned, scratched his armpits, and belched noisily. 'A man always feels better for a full stomach.'

'Your black mood has gone, then? Driven away by nothing more elaborate than bread, cheese and ale?'

'Aye. Perhaps, indeed, it was caused by nothing more fancy than hunger. Hunger's a dreadful scourge, master. Though I could be happier about this whole business. I wish I'd had an onion. Not that that's what I'm unhappy about. The other business, I meant. Did your old granny never say that someone had walked over her grave? Well, that was exactly how I felt this morning, and the thought of it is still with me, aye, and likely to spoil my temper the rest of the day, I fear.'

'Well then, why don't you take a stroll, get some fresh air, have a friendly talk with everyone you meet?'

'But aren't you wanting me with you?'

'Oh, everyone will be so busy enjoying themselves

today that they won't want to be bothered with questions.'

Clement grinned broadly, thanked Martin profusely, and made his way back into the kitchen. Martin watched him go, then went into the great hall, to seek out Sir George. He found him with the other two commissioners, finishing breakfast.

'Ah, Martin, glad to see you. Anything special planned for today, have you?'

'Nothing, Sir George. That is, unless you have any tasks for me?'

'Not at all. I don't know about the rest of you, but I'm quite looking forward to enjoying myself today. Something less onerous than thinking about murders and knives and what have you.' He looked at the others.

Timmons shrugged. 'We don't really seem to have done very much hard work thus far,' he said frankly. 'Still, perhaps a change of pace will jog our minds, point us towards the truth.'

Killane smiled gently. 'I confess it's many years since I participated in a Maying,' he told them. 'But let us neither forget why we were sent here, nor yet be too harsh on ourselves for heeding the drum and flute. Bear in mind that it was at this festival last year that Master Wood met his death. Who is to say that the circumstances of the festival had no relevance to the killing? Possibly if we keep our wits about us, we may spot something that will direct us to the guilty man.'

Sir George nodded approval. 'That's the thing! Business and pleasure both, eh? So, you can take yourself off for the rest of the day with a clear conscience, Martin.'

'I was wanting a word in private, if it were not inconvenient, Sir George.'

'Oh?'

'Nothing of immediate urgency,' Martin hastened to say, 'nor anything that has a bearing on our duty here. A family matter, so to speak.'

'Ah. Right, I'll be with you at once. Excuse me, gentlemen.' And he nodded to Timmons and Killane, and levered himself to his feet. 'Carry on, Martin, and I'll follow.'

Martin made his way out into the courtyard, which was already quite busy.

'Too crowded for privacy,' grunted Sir George. 'Let's take a walk behind the house,' and he set off across the bridge, and turned off the road that led to the tiny hamlet. 'Rabbit warren's over there,' he told Martin, waving a hand. 'Had some good sport there the other day, pity you didn't join us.' He stopped, and turned to look at Martin. 'Now then, young fellow, what's the trouble, then?'

'It's a delicate matter, I fear.'

'Ahah. Girl, is it? Well, you've asked the right man –'

'Good Lord, no, Sir George. It concerns Master Wood, and his untimely death.'

'Oh? Then why did you tell me it was a personal matter?'

Martin gave an embarrassed smile. 'It is a personal matter, in a sense at least. And I did not wish to make it too public, without first telling you, and getting your opinion of it.'

'I see. In that case, you'd better tell me, hadn't you?'

Martin stared at his boots. 'I have to say that it may be nothing much more than servants' gossip. Well, then. When I was speaking to Martha – she's one of the cooks here – she mentioned that Lady Kyme had been very upset by Wood's death. Now, in the circumstances, that would have been unremarkable, for the murder was unsettling enough in all conscience, and so I thought nothing more about it. Then Fortunato made some observation as to Lady Kyme always having a friendly word for Wood, though he was but a merchant. That sounded a trifle odd, so when I spoke to Bertram I made a point of asking him about it. He said that he, too, had thought Lady Kyme had – I don't know – had taken something more of an interest in Wood than he, Bertram, I mean to say, would have thought usual.'

'Or proper?'

'As to that, I couldn't say. Bertram strenuously maintained that there had been no impropriety, and no opportunity for any. As I say, it's the sort of thing any servant might well say. You know yourself how they gossip, invent scurrilous tales, or little intrigues, about masters and mistresses. But it bothered me, I confess. It isn't always nonsense that comes out of the kitchen.'

Sir George found a branch at a convenient height, crossed his arms over it, and rested his head on them. 'Let me see if I have this right. You're suggesting that there may have been some intrigue involving Wood and Lady Kyme. Lord Kyme finds out that Wood's put the horns on him, so he kills him – no, for Kyme did not leave the room – well, then, he has him killed, perhaps by one of the servants, Harry or someone. That it?'

'I'm certainly not suggesting anything of the sort, Sir George,' said Martin carefully. 'But I did want you to know what I'd heard, vague though it may be, and tell me what your opinion may be, before I noised it more generally abroad.'

'You did quite right to do so. Yes, if it's anything more

than servants' talk, there might be something very significant about it.' Sir George frowned. 'What I can't see is, if Kyme had anything to do with it, why the devil did he ask my lord Kemp to send us out here? You'd think he would wish to keep things as quiet as possible. I should hazard a guess that it's nothing more than gossip, myself. Still, when a man's lying dead, we can't simply ignore something like this.' He sighed loudly. 'The thing is, how do I put it to Lord Kyme?'

'Put what to me, Sir George?' came Kyme's voice from behind them.

They spun round, to see Kyme not ten feet away, an amused look on his face.

'You look like a couple of conspirators, seeking privacy in the woods for their plot. Not been poaching my rabbits, have you?'

Sir George laughed. 'Hardly, my lord. No, it was a delicate matter we wished to speak of.'

'Oh? And it involves me? That sounds like something I should know more about.'

Sir George shrugged. 'We had all but concluded that it was some servants' tale, some kitchen scandal.'

'Touching this matter of Master Wood?' Kyme looked serious now.

Sir George nodded.

'Then perhaps you ought to share it with me. As I've already told you, I'll do anything within my power to bring his murderer to justice.'

'I believe you would, my lord. Very well, then, as you insist upon it, let me ask you this. Did you know Wood, other than in the line of business? Had you ever met him before he started bringing his wares to Kyme?'

'Why do you ask that?' Kyme tried to make it sound

sprightly, but only succeeded in sounding guilty, to Martin's ear at any rate.

'I have my reasons.'

Kyme thought for a moment. 'I will say this. I had no dealings with him that might have had any significance as far as his death goes. That satisfy you?'

Sir George drew himself up to his full height. 'I fear not, my lord. I must ask you again. Did you know Wood, or anything of him, apart from your dealings with him here?'

Kyme kicked a pebble angrily. 'You'll not repeat this?' he asked.

'Not if it really has no bearing on the matter, no. But I cannot make any promises until I hear your tale.'

'That's fair enough.' Kyme glanced at Martin.

Martin said, 'I'll take a stroll, my lord, with your permission, to look at the rabbits.'

'You'll stay here,' Sir George told him. To Kyme, he added, 'Martin has uncovered what few facts we know about this sorry business. It's only right that he should hear this. His discretion may be relied upon, I'll vouch for that.'

'Very well.' Kyme cleared his throat. 'If you really must know, then, Wood was my wife's brother.'

'Good God!' Sir George did not bother to hide his astonishment.

'Or, to be strictly accurate, her half-brother. Same father, different mothers.' Kyme looked around for a place to sit, found one, and settled down, waving to the others to do the same. 'My wife's father was a wealthy man,' he continued, 'had lands five or six miles off. Well, he didn't marry until fairly late in life, and you know how it is. Wood was a by-blow, a bastard, if you want to put it bluntly. My wife's father provided for him, saw that his mother had enough money, and all the rest. Then he married my wife's mother, and my wife came along, some fifteen years after Wood. There were no other children, so he was naturally a little concerned as to what would happen to the estate.'

Sir George nodded. A bastard could not inherit, and although a daughter could, yet no man would wish to leave all his estate to a woman, if there were any alternative, for the potential for catastrophe was too great for comfort.

'Then, of course, she married me,' said Kyme, 'so that was fine. When he died – God rest him – the lands became part of Kyme.'

'And Wood?'

'Oh, by that time he was a grown man, and doing quite well in business. The old man had not had to support him for years, though I'm sure he would have done so had he been asked. He did continue an allowance to Wood's mother, up until he died – his wife knew nothing of it, I might add. And later, I continued the allowance, until the old lady died.'

'And when was that?'

'Oh, ten, twelve years ago? Something like that. It was my wife's father's expressed wish that I carry on making the payments, out of the revenues from his lands. It wasn't a large amount, just something for extra comforts. And Wood himself was also helping to support her by then.'

'And the arrangement was all quite amicable?'

'Oh, yes.'

'And that's how you came to deal with Wood?'

Kyme nodded. 'When he started in business, importing

rarities, he made me a present of a little monkey, the cousin of my wife's current pet, you'll have seen the creature? Well, I was so taken with it that I visited his premises, and that was the start of it.'

'And your dealings were business and nothing else?'

'Just so.' Kyme hesitated. 'He didn't come here very often. It was a bit awkward, under the circumstances, as you'll imagine readily enough. But, when he did come here, we made him welcome. He charged me a fair price for whatever I bought, didn't try to trade on the family connection in any way. Nor did he ever ask for money, except in the way of business, that is. Had he done so, I'd have given him a loan, or a gift, and thought nothing of it, glad to help. But he didn't, and I didn't offer. His business was a successful one, after all.'

'I see. And – how can I put this – Wood never tried to take advantage of his family connection in a more subtle way? He was never insolent, or anything of that sort?'

Kyme shook his head. 'I'd not have stood for anything of that sort, be he my wife's half-brother or not. No, he was always very civil, respectful. As I say, it was awkward for him – and for us, let's be honest – and that's why he came here so rarely.'

'And did anyone else at Kyme know anything of this?'

Kyme shook his head quickly.

'Sure?'

'As sure as I can be. I think I'd have known had there been any giggling behind hands, or anything of that sort, and I'd have put a stop to it pretty quick. But, if anyone knew, they didn't say. Why should they, after all? They'd probably think just as I do, that it's one of those things. Unless they had nothing better to do than gossip, and, as I say, I wasn't aware of any nonsense of that sort.'

'Well, I have to say thank you for your readiness to let us know about this,' said Sir George. 'I'm sorry for causing you any distress, I'm sure.'

'Oh, think nothing of it. But now you can understand why I'm so keen to bring Wood's murderer to justice. My wife was very upset about it. She liked the man, and so did I, for that matter. Had it not been for the absence of a wedding ceremony, I'd have owned him as my brother, and been proud to do so.' Kyme stood up. 'I'm only sorry that this doesn't help you at all.'

'It does eliminate one false scent, at any rate.'

'Yes, I suppose so. Well, I'm off. I'll see you at the festivities, later on?'

Sir George nodded. Kyme set off back towards the house.

'Well, Martin? That sort things out to your taste?'

'I think it probably does. As you said, there was no reason for Lord Kyme to have called us in, had he been personally involved. And the relationship with Wood does go far towards explaining why he's so anxious to bring Wood's killer to justice.'

'His explanation was good enough for me, at least.' Sir George got to his feet. 'You'll be attending the feast?'

'I was hoping to sit in Wood's place, and see what I can see.'

'Excellent notion. See you later, then.'

Martin sat for a time, turning the matter over in his mind, then gave it up. He got to his feet, and followed Kyme and Sir George back to the house.

As the morning wore on, the weather improved, but Martin's mood worsened rather noticeably. He spent some time wandering round the courtyard, aimlessly. Clement's mumbled remarks about Father Gerald and witches and warlocks, still bothered him, for all that he had dismissed them out of hand at the time.

By contrast, Clement grew more and more cheerful as it got closer to noon, and he eventually told Martin not to be so miserable, and in so many words.

'Easier said than done,' said Martin. He hesitated a moment, then added, 'We have at least an explanation for one puzzle. Wood was Lady Kyme's half-brother, wrong side of the blanket.'

Clement whistled. 'That accounts for her favouring him, then? And there was you and those other ill-bred churls thinking it was something else. The mind never rises above the cod-piece, with some folk. Well, that lets my lord out, doesn't it? He'd have no reason to be jealous of his brother-in-law, whichever side of the blanket he was.' And Clement went off, singing happily to himself.

Lord Kyme had sent word to those gentlemen who had been guests at Kyme the previous year, and these were now starting to arrive. Martin's gloom was deepened yet further by the reflection that any of these men could easily have killed Wood, improbable though it seemed that they should do so. He could at least try to establish whether any of the guests had left the table at last year's meal, but it was pointless to look for any assistance from Ralph, for the kitchens were, if anything, even busier and noisier than the courtyard. He looked round for Fortunato, and found him seated on a barrel, staring at the human pyramid.

'Fascinating, is it not?' asked Fortunato, with a wave at the tumblers. 'There seems an almost magical attraction to the sight of someone else working, even though the work be of the most undemanding sort. But, good Master Clerk, I can see that these drolleries are nothing more than an irritation just now, for you have a serious look about you. Can Fortunato possibly be of any help? It is, after all, my job to relieve gloom, to cheer up those afflicted by a melancholy turn of mind.'

'These gentlemen who are just now arrived, were all of them here last year?'

Fortunato nodded. 'So far as I can recall. The same old crowd as at all these affairs, as one might say.'

'I don't expect you noticed if any of them chanced to leave the hall at any point during the meal?'

'I should think not.' Fortunato laughed. 'You know well enough how these things are – the clients hang on their patron's every word. If one should need to go out to relieve himself, the others lose no opportunity to put in a good word on his behalf – I don't think! So they stay at the table, and either drink a lot less of someone else's ale than they'd really like to, or else shuffle in their seats a good deal.'

Martin nodded. He had seen enough of great men's households to know that this cynical view of things was not too far from the truth. One thing about the reply surprised him, though. 'Clients and patrons? You sound as if you've had a good grounding in the classics.'

'I have Master Wood to thank for that. He had had a good education, and he wasn't too stuck-up to share what he knew.' Fortunato grew silent, and stared at the ground for a time, then cheered up slightly and took hold of Martin's hand, leading him to the village green, where the festivities now began in a halting fashion.

Despite the fact that the weather had improved as the morning wore on, so that the day was now quite pleasant, there seemed a general air of hesitation, if not actual gloom, an unspoken doubt as to the advisability of the proceedings. The only person who put any enthusiasm into dancing round the Maypole was Clement, who had by now quite recovered his usual good humour, and who clumsily attempted to induce the village girls to enjoy themselves, but without any great success.

When Ralph came out to inform Kyme that all was ready for the meal, Martin sought out Jack Miller, who was seated on a bucket in a corner of the courtyard, looking as if the merriment were not to his taste.

'Do you recall where you sat last year?' Martin asked without preamble. His head ached vilely and he was in no mood to waste words on Miller.

'No, not exactly.'

Martin turned to some of the other villagers. 'Do any of you recall where Master Wood was sitting?'

They did, and explained at some length. Miller – naturally – saw fit to disagree, and the resulting discussion made Martin's headache even worse. But at last there was some consensus, and Martin and Clement managed to occupy the two seats which Wood and Bertram had taken last year, or at least two seats very close to the right spot. To make it as authentic as possible, Martin put a few of the villagers between Clement and Miller, which pleased Clement, who had not relished the idea of sitting too close to a man whom he regarded, even on a very short acquaintance, as the most churlish of all the many churls he, Clement, had ever had the misadventure to encounter.

Martin made a point of asking the villagers to mention anything they might remember as to last year's events, but the sole response was a mumbled remark halfway through the meal about the fuss which Ralph's news had caused.

As the proceedings drew to a close, Martin turned to

Clement and asked, 'Have some of these tumblers disappeared?'

Clement looked round carefully. 'They were all here for their set-piece,' he said, 'but now two of them, the two older men, have gone.'

Martin nodded. The six tumblers had formed their human pyramid soon after the start of the meal, and attracted some fitful applause, but now only the four younger men were left in the hall, doing handstands, or leaping over one another's backs. That would need looking into, for if the two older men had been outside last year as well, they might have noticed something. Martin made a mental note to question the two men who had left, and to insist on an answer this time.

The meal came to an end, and the bulk of the villagers began to drift away, seemingly not sorry that the festivities, if that was the right word, were over for that particular year. Martin moved closer to Miller, who had clearly been taking full advantage of Kyme's hospitality.

'Is all as it was last year?'

Miller rubbed his bleary eyes, and looked round. 'Yes. I suppose so. That's to say, nobody's been killed this year, have they? But apart from that, yes, all's pretty well the same.'

Martin looked for confirmation at the other few villagers who remained round about, but none could recall anything significant. And with that, though it added nothing to what he already knew, Martin had to be content. He caught Clement's eye, and, after thanking Miller and the others, went outside.

'Nothing worth hearing there, master.'

'No. But we must have a talk with those tumblers,' and Martin set off for the stables.

As before, they found the tumblers inside there, along with the rest of the entertainers, eating, drinking, and generally enjoying themselves, despite the somewhat unsavoury surroundings. There was an uneasy silence as Martin walked in, though, just as there had been on the last occasion.

'Sorry to disturb you again,' Martin told them. He glanced around, and spotted one of the older tumblers who had left the great hall during the meal. 'It was really you I wanted to speak to, good sir.'

The man looked apprehensive, and Martin fancied he could hear a subdued sigh of relief from those not selected for his special attentions.

'Don't worry,' he tried to reassure the man, 'it's only one or two more questions. Now, your performance starts with a spectacular set-piece, with all of you standing on one another's backs, is that not so?'

'Right, sir.'

'But then for the rest of the time, the more active performance on the floor of the hall, it's just these younger men here?'

'You have it, sir. Tom and me, and the youngster –' the youngster was eighteen or so – 'we form the base, as you might call it, support the others, who, being younger, are that much lighter. But then, for the rest of the tricks, leap-frog and what have you, Tom and me are a bit old, joints a bit stiff, you might say, so we leave it to the youngsters. Right, Tom?'

Tom nodded approval of the explanation. 'Right, Peter.'

'And you did the same last year?'

'Aye.'

'And when you'd done, you went outside for a breath of air no doubt?'

'Aye.' It was out before Peter had time to think, and Tom shot him a glance that held no approval.

Martin said, 'I see. I did just wonder if, last year, you didn't go for a walk outside the walls? Someone mentioned that they'd seen you out in the courtyard, as if you were heading towards the village.'

'Oh? Did we, Tom? Do you recall?'

Tom scratched his head as an aid to thought. 'Can't say as I recollect, rightly.'

'I'm not concerned with where you went,' said Martin. 'There'll be no questions as to my lord's rabbits, or anything of that sort. But I would like to know.'

'Now you mention it, I think we took a walk outside. Yes, I'm sure we did. Was it a young gentleman who told you that, by any chance, sir? A fine-looking, well set up sort of young gentleman?'

'Yes, it was. He said he'd seen you, and thought you were going out for a walk.'

'You have it, sir. A walk, that's right, it being such a pleasant day.'

'And you didn't happen to see my lord's constable out for a walk?'

There was an uneasy laugh from the listeners at this. Tom frowned, but did not reply directly. Martin went on, 'I don't intend to cause trouble, but it would help me enormously if I could be sure as to where Harry Constable was that afternoon.' And he rattled his purse significantly.

Tom said, 'I do believe I spotted him out by the woods.'

'In the general direction of the rabbit warren?'

'Aye, happen it was.'

'And did he see you?'

The laughter was louder at this. Even Tom grinned as he answered, 'I don't believe he did, sir.'

'And when was this?' asked Martin.

Tom and Peter looked at each other and shrugged. 'We don't reckon time by the clock, sir,' said Peter. 'But we got back here as all the fuss was going on.'

'Master Wood's body had just been found, you mean?'

'Aye.'

'And was Harry still outside?'

'He was,' said Tom, and Peter nodded agreement.

Martin thanked them, and handed over a few coppers. He and Clement went out into the courtyard.

'I said Harry couldn't have anything to do with it,' said Clement confidently.

'We can't take things for granted. Hello, what's this?' and Martin nodded towards the main gate.

Clement looked, to see a horseman in livery come at full tilt over through the gateway, pull his horse up viciously, and threw the reins to a passing servant, before demanding, in a voice made harsh with dust, to see Lord Kyme. The servant stammered out some reply, pointing to the house, and the rider strode off to the door.

'Looks like a messenger,' said Clement, looking wise.

'Well observed. And the message is an urgent one by the look of him.'

'Shall we go inside, take a look, see what's to do?'

There seemed no reason why they should not go inside, for if the message were a private one, they would be told as much soon enough. If not, then it might be something Sir George should know. Martin started towards the door, but before he reached it Ralph came out, and hurried into the wing which contained Sir George's room.

'It looks as if it may concern their honours the commissioners, then,' Martin said. He drew Clement to the side of the door, and waited. After a very short while, Ralph emerged again, followed, as Martin had expected, by Sir George, then Timmons and Killane. It looked serious, but they did not stop to tell Martin to go in with them, so he hesitated, until Ralph came out yet again, looked round – for it was growing dark by this time – and beckoned to Martin.

'Master Byrd, my lord thinks you should hear the news as well,' he said, and led Martin indoors. Clement marched boldly after his master, staring Ralph, who raised an eyebrow at him, out of countenance.

Sir George, Lord Kyme and the others were seated round a table, talking to the rider who had just come in.

'Ah, Martin, Clement. Sit down.' Sir George waved a hand. 'My clerk,' he explained to the messenger, who nodded. 'Well, Martin, the storm's broken at last.'

'Oh?' Martin tried to make it sound as if he understood Sir George's cryptic remark perfectly.

'My lord Suffolk has fled,' the messenger explained.

'Fled? When? And where to?'

'Yesterday. That much is certain,' the messenger told him. 'As to where he may be right now, God alone knows. Rumour says France, and rumour is probably right. He seems to have fled England altogether, rather than face his enemies, that much at any rate is certain.'

'Something of the sort has been in the wind for a while,' said Martin.

The messenger nodded gravely, and Kyme grunted assent.

'This is all very well,' said Sir George, 'but it doesn't tell us what to do next.'

'It doesn't need to, as far as I'm concerned,' said Timmons drily.

'Oh?'

'My family's fortunes are bound up very closely with those of Suffolk, and have been for some years past. If he's fallen from favour, then I shall probably have to retreat to my father's house and grow cabbages.'

'Come now,' said Sir George, 'it may not be that bad. You'll still be a judge, unless things go very badly.'

'Aye. But –' and Timmons shrugged and left the rest, concerning his quiet ambition – which had never been made public, and now never would be – to be more than a judge one day, unspoken.

'To immediate matters, then,' said Sir George.

The messenger stood up. 'My most pressing task, if I may impose on your lordship to the extent of a fresh horse, is to continue to spread the word. I can be in Norwich before it gets too dark to ride.'

'It's nearly that now,' said Kyme doubtfully. 'You'll not stay here tonight, continue tomorrow after a decent night's sleep?'

'By your leave, my lord, no, I'd sooner get on to Norwich. I'll find a bed there easily enough,' and he said his farewells and left.

'And now, my lord,' Sir George resumed, 'what is your opinion as to the situation in these parts?'

'Well, there'll be some changes, obviously. Assuming Suffolk has gone, and you can't always be certain. But news travels slowly in the countryside, and the ordinary folk don't trouble too much about doings at court. The gentry, now.' He rubbed his chin. 'There may be one or two old scores settled, you know how it is. But, that apart, there should be no real danger. This place is proof against all but the most determined siege, if it came to that, and I don't think it will. I can't see there being any concerted unrest in these parts, whatever individual families may think of Suffolk.'

'So you don't need us here, for the next few days at least?'

'No.'

'Right, so what's our best course of action? Timmons?'

'I'm for returning to London, Sir George, to see what can be done to save the situation.'

'Master Killane?'

Killane gave his dreamy smile, and stared at the ceiling. 'I recall a very similar state of affairs – oh, donkey's years ago, now, of course. Me and another young chap, we were busy with some matter or another, can't remember the details, and word came, some upset at court, some – what shall we say? – subtle shift of power, close to the King, very similar to the present situation, in fact. Well, nothing would do for this other chap but to ride off that day, see what was to be done. But I was more circumspect, even in those days, and I couldn't for the life of me see that there was anything I could do, I wasn't important enough to have any effect, you see. And, when I did return, sure enough, there was my friend, or his head, rather, grinning at me from a pikestaff on London Bridge. Frequently thought about that, when I've been tempted to act too hastily.'

'I see,' said Sir George.

'Is that true?' Timmons demanded.

Killane smiled at him. 'Of course. Would I make up something like that? I was merely trying to point out that he who acts in haste sometimes has no leisure in which to repent. You have relatives at court?'

Timmons nodded.

'Sensible folk, are they? Know what's what?'

Timmons nodded again.

'Well, then,' said Killane, 'what could you do to save the day that they could not? Trust to their judgement, as you'd wish them to trust to yours were the position reversed. And if, God forbid, the worst happens and it's devil take the hindmost, then you're far better off out of it.'

Timmons thought this over, then gave a final nod. 'You're quite right, sir. The wisdom of experience has a lot to recommend it.'

'So,' said Sir George, 'we stay here, eh? Until the situation becomes clearer, at least. With your permission, that is, my lord.'

'By all means,' said Kyme. 'Glad to have someone to talk to at a troublesome time such as this may prove to be.' He stood up. 'I don't know about you gentlemen, but I've been given a good deal to think about, so I believe I'll go either to think, or to have an early night, with a view to thinking tomorrow.'

The others seemed to consider this sensible, and there were subdued good nights all round.

When they reached their room, Clement, who had listened to all that had gone on without understanding more than half of it, was inclined to ask Martin a few questions, but Martin too had much to think about, and waved his servant away. 'Tomorrow, Clement,' said he, 'tomorrow.' And Clement had to be satisfied with that.

Ten

$\mathfrak{M}$artin slept badly, and it seemed as if Clement, who usually slept like a log, had the same difficulty, for Martin heard him shuffling, and turning over, and cursing under his breath all night long. At cock-crow, Martin decided that he had had more than enough of all this. He rose, and went out into the courtyard, where he plunged his head into a bucket of icy water from the well before taking a stroll to the main gate.

When he returned to the room, feeling considerably fresher, he found Clement sitting up, his head in his hands.

'A nice wash in cold water will wake you up,' Martin advised.

Clement shuddered. 'I prefer to wake up slowly and naturally, master.' He stretched and yawned. 'Might you perhaps be in a better mood, and ready to answer a few questions now?'

'I'll do my best.'

'Master Timmons was very concerned about getting back to London. That'll be because his family's fortunes are linked with those of my lord Suffolk, so I understand that. But why then is Master Killane urging caution?'

'You heard his little tale,' said Martin.

'I did, but I can't say I really saw the point of it. A man like Master Timmons, rich, powerful, why shouldn't he try to hold on to what he has? Very sensible, I should say.'

'True, but it's equally sensible to be cautious as to how he goes about it. After all, Suffolk was even richer and more powerful than Master Timmons, and yet from what we heard yesterday, it seems certain that Suffolk has fled, and that means that his enemies now have the upper hand – or at any rate, Suffolk believes that they have. Even if they had not, if Suffolk were mistaken, then his flight will mean that those enemies seize their chance. They'll point to the flight as conclusive proof that Suffolk was guilty.'

'But of what? It's that that's really got me puzzled. I don't see how a man like Suffolk, a man who had the King's ear, a man almost as powerful as the King himself – if not, indeed, more powerful, as I seem to recollect you yourself saying – well, I don't see how a man like that can be accused in a vague way. What are his enemies claiming that he's guilty of?'

'Why, of anything that comes to mind, misuse of his official position, for one thing, plotting to take over the throne, perhaps. His behaviour has been arrogant enough for a case to be made out there, if you ask me. But that's the beauty of the fact that Suffolk's fled, from his enemies' viewpoint, for now they don't have to be specific, they merely have to say that the flight indicates a guilty conscience, and let rumour and suspicion – and, God knows, there are plenty of both at court – do the rest. In fact, the less they say, the more will rumour exaggerate Suffolk's crimes. Yes, there will indeed be lots of old scores settled, as Lord Kyme puts it, you may depend on that. Perhaps not out here, but in London, not with a sword but with a writ, or a few words in the ear of the

Lord Chancellor – whoever that is at the time. Those who were Suffolk's closest associates, the most powerful men in the land, will now be out of favour, and lucky to escape with their heads, in the most literal sense.'

'And here? Lord Kyme said he thought things would not be too bad, yet I thought he was Suffolk's man too.'

Martin nodded. 'He is – or was. But the court is the heart of power, and hence of intrigue. These local land-owners, Lord Kyme and the others, may well depend on the great men, Suffolk and his like, for those things connected with the court, a position for a younger son, let's say, an advantageous marriage for a daughter, but as far as the ordinary business of living from day to day is concerned, they are independent of London, and the great men who form the court.' He smiled.

'Master?'

'Oh, I was just thinking, I made so bold as to mention something about ambition, and being at court in London, to Lord Kyme the other day, and his reply was that he was content to be out of the way here, that he desired neither the sort of greatness that Suffolk had, nor the disasters that might befall. Almost prophetic, in a way. Though, to be fair, this business of Suffolk has been simmering for some time now.'

'He was felt to be too big for his breeches, eh?'

'Oh, both Suffolk and his breeches were big enough. It was more a case of other men, almost as big as he, and with equally big breeches, thinking that they would quite like to stand before the fire of state and warm their backsides. And Suffolk stood in the way.'

'It's at times like this that you could almost be glad that you're so poor that nobody would ever think to envy you,' said Clement. 'But tell me, master, how does your family – how do you yourself stand, now that Suffolk has fallen?'

'Do I detect a faint note of anxiety?'

'Concern, master. Concern for your welfare, as befits an old and faithful servant, one looking out for the interests of the young master that he's served so long, so faithfully, and for so very little in the way of reward.'

'H'mm. Well, fear not. It's true enough that I got my post thanks to a word from a friend of my father's in Lord Kemp's ear, or perhaps the ear of a man who had the ear of Lord Kemp. Such is the way of things, and will be for some time yet, I fancy. But there's nothing to say that Kemp will fall just because Suffolk does, and even should he do so, then it doesn't mean that everyone who owes their position to him will similarly be regarded with disfavour, for the court is too big for that sort of thing – if everyone who owed their position to patronage were removed, there'd simply be nobody left to run things. No, we humbler folk are fairly safe, as a general rule. Indeed, there are many instances of a great man's secretary transferring his allegiance to the equally great man who's just replaced his master. Aye, and serving him just as well.'

Clement clicked his tongue and shook his head disapprovingly.

'As I say, that's the way of things.'

'No, it was just regret, master, regret that I never learned to read and write. Who can tell, I might have been secretary to some great man, and thus able to make a fortune whilst keeping my head on my shoulders. Trust those fellows, they know how to work the trick!' He stretched again. 'I wonder if we can get into the kitchen yet? There should be someone around in there who could fix us up with some grub.'

'I'm delighted to see that the momentous doings and occasional concomitant tragedies of puissant individuals are not weighing too heavily on your mind.'

'What? Oh, I see what you mean. No, no, I can do nothing about those things, so there's no point worrying about them, is there? There is just one little thing that puzzles me in all this, and that is, how will it affect our job here?'

'That's something that I've wondered about too,' said Martin. 'I can't see why it should alter anything, the law should take its course whatever happens at court. But that's a simpleton's view. If the matter ever gets as far as bringing a charge against a specific person, we may well find a writ of supersedeas arrives from the Lord Chancellor – whoever he may be,' he added with a grin.

'Interest having been made on behalf of the guilty man?'

'The accused man,' Martin corrected. 'But, yes, more or less. If the man who eventually stands accused happens to have a friend who has influence, then the matter could be taken before Kemp, or whoever may be Chancellor, and the man never even come to trial.'

Clement scratched his head. 'But then, it would alter, depending on who had Kemp's ear. Or the ear of whoever sits on the Woolsack.'

'You mean, the same man might be found guilty, or else walk free, depending on whether his family supported Suffolk, or whoever may take Suffolk's place? Yes, that's a fair enough way of looking at it. And by the same token, if Suffolk had not fled, then the same man could hang or go free, depending on whether his family inclined to Suffolk or otherwise.'

'Well, it's not right, is it?' demanded Clement.

'No, I would not for one moment pretend that it is. But remember that, by and large, the judges are honest men, if you don't count these petty local chieftains, who run things as they please. It's this selection of jurors, and writs of this and that from whoever may be Lord Chancellor, that spoil things. If we could actually name a man we thought guilty, then he'd be convicted, I'm sure, barring direct intervention from London. And just at the moment, I think Kemp probably has other fish to fry. So, if we could move quickly, we might conclude this business satisfactorily.'

'But, master, as yet we have not the slightest idea as to who may have done it.'

'That is one small, but very serious, drawback,' Martin admitted. 'Now, you said something about visiting the kitchen?'

They found a few sleepy cooks and scullions, and managed to get some breakfast. There was a certain amount of talk among the kitchen staff as to what might happen now that Suffolk was gone, and Martin's opinion was asked on more than one point, but he could not tell them much more than he had told Clement.

As they were finishing, there was a slight commotion near the door, and Martin looked up, to see Sir George come hesitantly into the kitchen.

'No,' said Sir George as Martin made to rise, 'please don't get up. I couldn't sleep, turning this business over and over in my mind, so I thought I'd see if I couldn't get an early breakfast.'

Made bold by this unexpectedly human admission, Martin asked, 'What course of action do you propose to take?'

'Damned if I know,' said Sir George frankly. 'Whilst

I've been quite happy to let you look into things thus far – and you've not done badly, I'll say that, even if we haven't actually managed to produce a name yet – this business of Suffolk's fall from favour does change things quite considerably. I don't really fancy sitting around doing nothing, not when there are stirring events befalling in London, but I think Mr Justice Killane is right about this sort of upset, it's far safer not to be too close to the King when things go wrong in this sort of way, for those who are too involved in something like this are most at risk. All we can really do is wait, and that's one of the hardest things of all to do well.' He shrugged, and applied himself to his bread and cheese.

Everyone at Kyme seemed stricken by the same black mood. When Sir George had finished eating, he, Martin and Clement went into the great hall, to see if the others were up and about. There was no sign of Lord Kyme or his wife, and such servants as were wandering about the place were morose and silent.

Timmons appeared, but he ate little, and then asked if Sir George intended doing anything special that day. When Sir George gave a non-committal reply, Timmons excused himself, saying that he had much to think over, and would be in his room if anyone needed him.

Killane appeared even later, complaining of a headache. He ate nothing at all, and he, too, soon sought the peace and quiet of his room.

'This is worse than useless,' Sir George complained. 'We can do nothing about the larger matter, so what about this business of Wood's murder? Haven't got very far there, have we? Bertram inherited his money, but wishes he hadn't. Young Middleham's knife was used, but Middleham didn't know Wood. It gets darker, not lighter, the more you think about it.'

'It occurs to me,' said Clement, 'that it might not have been a man who killed Wood at all.'

'Oh, not your witches and wizards!' said Martin.

'Oh, no. I meant the bear.'

Martin and Sir George looked blank.

Clement explained, 'Someone said that there was a chap with a dancing bear here at Kyme last year, though I haven't seen him this. I thought perhaps it might have been the bear that killed Master Wood.'

'Nonsense!' Sir George did not trouble to hide his scorn at this. 'A bear might claw you, or maybe crush the life out of you. It wouldn't take a knife from its belt and stab you.'

'It occurs to me,' said Martin, 'that I heard some tale of some townspeople who tried a pig.'

'A pig?'

'Yes, it had killed a small child, rolled over on top of it, as I recall, and they tried it for murder, found it guilty, and hanged it.'

'Where was this?' Sir George wanted to know.

'I can't quite recollect. France, perhaps? Or Germany?'

'Oh, well.' Sir George was nothing if not an Englishman. 'You know what those fellows are. Do anything over there. Damned if I know why we persist in hanging on to Calais. Wouldn't occur to anyone to think about it, were it not for some tanner's bastard a couple of centuries ago.'

'But the point I was making,' said Martin, feeling this was going to be an uphill task, 'is that animals do kill people, quite by accident.'

'Chap I knew was gored by a bull,' said Clement helpfully. 'Nice chap, too. Kept an inn. Had a pretty young wife,' he added, a faraway look in his eye.

'Well, then,' said Sir George. 'I can't see it, but let's pretend for a moment that there had been two sheer accidents that day. One, the bear finds the knife. Two, it kills Wood. Now, that's fair enough as far as it goes, apart from the sheer implausibility of the whole business, but you must answer me this. Why did the maid not see the bear? You could hardly miss a damn great bear, however distraught you might be. I don't profess to be any sort of an expert, but I'd have thought that the smell of blood would have caused the bear to attack the body, or at the very least lurk round it, sniffing it and so forth. And, for good measure, tell me just where the bear's owner might have been, while all this was going on?'

Clement shrugged his shoulders.

'No,' said Sir George, 'I don't think that takes us much further. Indeed, I could almost wish that my lord Kemp would send word that the matter has been moved to London, and that I needn't think about it any longer. I –' and he was interrupted by a clatter of hooves outside, and harsh commands shouted at some tardy servant.

'By Heaven, I really believe Kemp has sent a messenger!' said Sir George. 'If he has, then it's the first time my prayers have ever been answered so completely. Or so promptly. Or at all! I'll burn a few candles if it is so, I can tell you!'

But it was not a messenger from the Lord Chancellor, bearing that writ of supersedeas which Sir George so earnestly desired, who entered the room a moment later. It was a short, sturdy man in some livery that Martin could not place, though Sir George gave a grunt of recognition.

'Sheriff's man, are you?' he asked the messenger.

'I am, sir. Sir George Maryon?'

Sir George nodded.

'You've heard the news of my lord Suffolk, I understand? My lord sheriff is uncertain as to how the townspeople will react when they hear, as they will before very long, and he wondered if you and the other gentlemen would like to move to Norwich – we'll find you suitable quarters – in case there's any sort of unrest.'

Sir George did not have to think more than a moment before nodding his agreement. 'A good notion. We don't want any of the sort of thing that has already happened in Portsmouth, or London. A show of strength, that's the best course of action. Are you wanting to get back, or will you wait until we can make everything ready? It shouldn't take long.'

The messenger elected to wait. Sir George asked one of the servants to seek out Lord Kyme, whilst Martin and Clement alerted Timmons and Killane to what was going on.

By the time that Martin had found Timmons and returned to the great hall with him, Lord Kyme was in there, looking grave, and saying, 'Yes, I think it's best if you do go. If there's any danger at all, it'll come from the mob in the town, not out here in the wilds.'

'You're certain you'll be safe enough here?' asked Sir George.

'Quite certain. You'll have seen for yourselves that the place is well nigh impregnable, and I have Harry and his men-at-arms about the place. If there were any unrest, we'd soon put it down, believe me.'

'Very well, my lord. Clement, will you stir up those idle servants of ours, and make sure that all's ready as soon as possible?'

'I'll supervise it myself, your honour.'

Clement, who had always persisted in thinking himself a cut – if not two – above Sir George's own servants, used his voice and his fists to good effect, and soon had things moving. But the necessary preparations nevertheless took some time, so that it was early afternoon before they set off, and they were obliged to move at the pace of the horses and mules which bore the heavy baggage.

It was getting dark by the time they reached Norwich, but there were still small groups of people standing about on the outskirts of the town, and even more folk in the market place, staring at the little procession as it passed the new church of St Peter, and moved towards the castle.

'It looks as if word has reached them,' Martin told Clement, nodding at those who stood watching. 'They should be indoors at their supper, by rights.'

'Aye. They look as if they're a bit more alert than your ordinary churl, as if they take an interest in what goes on in the wider world, and that's why they want to know just what's what right now. Comes of living in a prosperous town.' Clement raised a thumb in the direction of the new church. 'All built on corn, so they tell me. Another thing, you'll always find that the women in these rich towns are more – how shall I put this? – friendly, so to speak. Comes of having money, makes them more independent of their menfolk. You notice that particularly where the women earn their own wages. Nottingham is noted for it, the lacemaking, you know. Makes them much more agreeable and willing.' He leered at the nearest young woman, who gave him a frightened look and raced off as fast as she could.

'Yes, I can see how it works,' said Martin.

'Usually, master, usually. In the general run of things.' He stared at the bulk of the castle which towered over them. 'Uninviting sort of place, this. I wonder what the grub's like? Mind you, these sheriffs and constables do themselves pretty well. Never known one of them to content himself with bread and cheese.'

The members of the special commission went to see the sheriff, leaving Martin with the other servants in the courtyard. Clement went off on his own, to see, he said, where the kitchens might be located. Martin could not very well give any orders as to the disposition of the horses and baggage until he heard from Sir George, so he waited rather uncomfortably outside for close to half an hour, before he was called in to see Sir George, who was seated in a small room off the great hall of the castle. Timmons and Killane were there as well, but there was no sign of the sheriff or any of his men.

'I've had a quick word with the sheriff,' Sir George told him, 'and there seems little danger, for tonight at any rate, so we'll just find somewhere to sleep, and see what tomorrow brings. We can have a longer talk then, plan what's best to do. So, find yourself a bed for the night.'

Martin nodded. 'No special instructions for me then, Sir George?'

'Not really. I rather suspect that all we'll really be needed for is to ride in the sheriff's train when he goes through the town, and look as fierce and forbidding as possible.' Sir George grinned. 'Put on a show for the benefit of those who might be disposed to roguery. Not that I imagine there'll be too many of them. Most of them here are solid citizens, with their fortunes in their businesses, and with little interest in the doings of such men as Suffolk, except insofar as the patronage of great men can be useful to them. And that being so, they'll simply look for a new patron.'

Martin nodded. 'And yet there are masterless men in every town, men who will take advantage of any twist and turn in the settled order of things to proclaim their own grievances, be they real or imagined. We saw that in Kent last year, and in London only lately. Doubtless my lord sheriff will be giving some thought to reinforcing his own troops, just in case. Well, if there's nothing further, I'll attend to the baggage and so forth.'

'Do that, would you? I fear that the quarters here will not be quite as luxurious as at Kyme, but that can't be helped.'

The quarters were, indeed, very inferior to those they had left. Martin and Clement were obliged to share a very poky room with two of Sir George's own servants, men of little learning and a coarse turn of phrase, and this irritated Clement immensely. The rest of the evening was occupied with transferring the baggage into the rooms allocated to them, so that they went hungry until supper time, when Clement was pleased to discover that, as he had hoped, the food, though not particularly dainty, was at least plentiful.

Eleven

Had you asked him about it afterwards, Martin could not have told you just how he had passed the remainder of that day. Sir George was busy talking with the sheriff and some of the town's dignitaries for most of the morning, and Martin was not invited to take part. It was not until almost noon that he was summoned into Sir George's presence. There was no sign of any of those men with whom Sir George had been speaking, and Martin was not asked to sit down.

'I'll be brief, Martin,' Sir George began. 'The state of things can be explained very easily. As you were saying yesterday, the sheriff is somewhat anxious lest there is any unrest here – though it's only an outside chance, we were all agreed on that – and accordingly is asking for extra men from some of the local nobles round about, to strengthen his own forces until things have become clearer.'

Martin nodded. Even as such a time as this, when there were dramatic changes close to the King, there was little real danger of serious unrest in rural areas. For one thing, news reached isolated places only slowly, so that by the time the ordinary farm labourer got to hear of any shift of power, such was occurring at the moment, it was very old news, the thing was over and done with, and had been for perhaps a couple of months.

Then again, events in London were a matter of indifference to country folk. And if by some chance an item of news did stir every last man in some tiny hamlet into a fury, what could they do, even acting all together? A dozen determined men might perhaps burn a field of corn, or cause some damage to the parish church, but that was all, and there would be little point their doing even that, for they would need the corn to feed themselves and their families. Finally, no hamlet was so isolated that it did not have its lord, and his overlord, with their constables and men-at-arms and sheriff's men at their backs, all ready with fist and foot, lash and gallows.

But things were not quite so settled once you came to a town of any size. There would be nobles, merchants, men who were in constant touch with their fellows in other towns, even London itself. News reached such men quickly, particularly if it touched upon their own interests, and it soon spread, first to the great men's servants, thence to the rest of the townsfolk, as like as not being exaggerated at every telling and re-telling, so that by the time it reached the poor in the crowded tenements, news had been subtly transmuted into its bastard cousin, rumour.

Then, the outlook of townspeople was radically different from that of countryfolk. Town dwellers formed groups with a community of interest, from the trade guilds down to the loose associations between the young apprentices. They would meet their fellows, discuss what might affect all of them, debate, argue amongst themselves. And if they perceived some danger that might affect each member of the group, they would not think twice about acting to counter it, as had happened quite often when the apprentice boys had some grievance, real or imagined, and went on the rampage through the streets.

There was also more potential to do damage in a town. The merchants' warehouses could be sacked or burned, taverns or private houses might be broken into, and the owners would not easily recognize the malefactors in a large group.

The last point, the sheer size of the mob, was perhaps the most significant. There were simply far more people to the square rood in a town than in the country, and that could present a real danger, particularly if the poor tenement dwellers took it into their heads to translate some grievance – of which they had plenty, in all conscience, and real enough to boot – into action. The typical town council feared the mob as it feared the Black Death.

Sir George went on, 'We'll stay here a day or so, show the flag, so to speak, until things are more settled.' He stood up. 'There's nothing vital that must be done at once, so you can come along with me, and we'll impress the people with the power of the law.'

This they proceeded to do, by standing outside the Castle, and make a great show of greeting the miserable looking men-at-arms who had been sent by the great men round about, who were now starting to arrive in little bunches, half a dozen here and there, in a score of different liveries. They looked miserable, most of them at least, because they had not in any sense volunteered for this task, but had been ordered to do it, and they were concerned lest there should be some actual danger to themselves. Only one or two of the younger men, who welcomed this change from the monotony of life in the fields, were free from the general melancholy.

Martin felt out of place. He could do nothing con-
structive, only stand next to Sir George and pretend that
he was part of the machinery of government, which was
true enough as far as it went, but it struck him as rather
pointless just at the moment. Still, he tried his best to
look grim and implacable in the King's name, and doubtless impressed some of the younger boys who gathered
outside the castle to gaze, open-mouthed, at the great
men. Clement was nowhere to be seen. He had made a
hearty breakfast, then vanished magically. Martin found
that could not in all conscience blame him for that. The
day dragged on, and somehow it came to the dinner
hour. Clement, as might be expected, showed up then
right enough, saying how hungry he was.

'Yes, it takes it out of you, keeping out of the way of any
work,' said Martin.

Clement looked hurt at this. 'Master, I've been out and
about in the town, trying to see what the mood of the
common folk might be. I think I can safely say that I've
called at every tavern, ale-house and knocking-shop in
the place.'

'Now, that's something I can believe.'

Clement looked hurt again. 'All in the line of duty,
master. Nothing more than that.'

'And what is it?'

'What's what? Oh, I see, their mood. Out and out
puzzlement, for the most part. I have been assured that
my lord of Suffolk is in France, that he is dead and his
head on a pike on London Bridge, and that he is alive
and well and waiting to confound his enemies. Even that
it's the King who is dead, and Suffolk is crowned in his
place.'

Martin nodded. 'Pretty much what you would expect,

in the circumstances. I might perhaps believe the first rumour, that he is in France, for that's the obvious place he would go, if he has fled, to seek the protection of the French King, or perhaps to plan his next move, for he . won't want to let go of what he had without a struggle.'

The day staggered on to a close, and although Martin had to admit that Clement's unfavourable opinion of their room-mates was a perfectly accurate one, he did not feel disposed to stay up doing nothing. As ill luck would have it, the others had had the same idea, so that when Martin sought his bed the room was already echoing to the sounds of loud snoring. Martin's rest was yet further disturbed when one of the sheriff's officers put his head round the door and asked if there was any space for a couple of the new recruits. Fortunately Clement and Sir George's two men, who rather resented having their sleep interrupted, were able to persuade him that there was not, and there were no further interruptions. Incredibly, once the door had closed after the interrupters, Martin, tired out by doing nothing in particular, did not even notice the snoring of his companions.

The following day looked set fair to be a repeat of the last. Martin, in no mood to be trifled with, told Clement that he must stay by his master's side. 'If I'm to be bored to tears, then you can be as well.'

Clement was at first inclined to grumble, but when he realized that all that would be required of him was to stand outside the castle, look important, and give occasional orders to the recruits, he threw himself into the task with a will.

Towards noon, a messenger, hot and dusty, rode up to the castle gate and asked to speak to the sheriff.

'Trouble?' said Clement.

'More news, I hope, instead of rumour.'

'No good news, by the look on his face, though. Shall we go in and see what's amiss?'

Martin could see no reason why they should not, so they went inside to look for Sir George, but he found them, taking Martin's arm and dragging him to a quiet spot. Clement trailed along after them, wondering what it was all about.

'It looks as if Suffolk's dead,' Sir George began without preamble.

'How?'

'Hanged, so they say. He was trying to get a ship to France, and apparently the ship's captain actually did the hanging.'

'I see.'

'Though I can't quite make out whether it was by the King's order, or what. He may have thought to advance himself by doing it, or simply been paying off some old score. If it was him, of course.'

'Any word on what the effects will be, or is it too early?'

'There's apparently great rejoicing in London, evidently they're not too sorry to see the last of Suffolk. But there is some talk of unrest in Kent, and it's there the danger may lie.'

Martin nodded. The men of Kent were not slow to voice their dissatisfaction with the state of things, and had already done so more than once just lately. If they now believed that their actions had resulted in the death of Suffolk, or at any rate been a contributory factor, they would be encouraged to try to do more. And, although Martin could sympathize up to a point with the bulk of their grievances, which were connected with the virtual breakdown of the legal system that he and Clement had remarked on earlier, that did not make the prospect of insurrection any more pleasant.

'Look here, Martin, the sheriff has enough men here now to curb any but the most determined riot, and I don't take that possibility seriously. If there's trouble, it'll almost certainly come in London, so I think we're as well heading back there, to see if we're needed. If there's any personal danger, either from the mob or from the other little matter, well, so be it, we'll just have to face that if it happens.'

'Very good, Sir George. Shall I give orders to make ready?'

'No. I don't know if that chap –' he evidently meant the messenger – 'has been to Kyme with the news, what with all the excitement I forgot to ask, and he's cleared off again. But I think Lord Kyme should hear of this as soon as possible, so you and Clement ride there at once, will you? I'll see that all's made ready here, and we'll meet you at Kyme as soon as may be possible, then we can all travel to London in a group. Safer that way.'

Martin nodded agreement, and he and Clement set off, and soon left the last houses of Norwich behind them. Once or twice they were stopped by farm workers, eager for any recent news of what might be going on. Most of these people assumed that anyone who had come from Norwich must know the inquirer's sons or brothers personally, and that caused some confusion and consequent delay. Still, these interruptions were not many in number, and Martin and Clement arrived at Kyme in the middle of the afternoon – or, as Clement would have it, just nicely in time for dinner – without any incident worthy of remark.

Harry, who was standing outside the main gate, raised a hand in greeting as they rode into view, and they slowed down as they reached him.

'A right old to-do, this, isn't it?' Harry asked, with a grin and a shrug of the shoulders to indicate his mixed emotions. 'But then, them as lives longest will see the most, as my old mother used to say.'

'I take it you've seen the most recent messenger, then?' asked Martin.

'That chap this morning, who said that Suffolk's been hung? Aye, we saw him.'

'Then anything we can say is not exactly fresh, I fear. Sir George wasn't sure whether or not you'd have heard, and sent us to let you know. There seems no likelihood of any unrest in Norwich, so Sir George intends to return to London, calling here first to collect the two of us, and also to have a word with Lord Kyme.'

Harry nodded sagely. 'Aye. It's probably best for each man to look to his own back-yard in times like these. No doubt there'll be a whole heap of things needing to be attended to in London, as a result of all this.'

'And not just in London, I fancy. How has Lord Kyme taken this latest news, or don't you know?'

'He hasn't left his own chamber much at all, ever since he heard. He'll have more to think over than most men, what with being so close to Suffolk, as it were.'

Martin could not refrain from thinking that it was every bit as likely that Kyme was packing his more portable – and more valuable – goods away into a travelling chest, ready for flight if things got too bad. Not that Martin or anyone else would have blamed him if that were so, it was far more sensible to flee than stay to be killed, and no man need be ashamed of saving his life.

Martin did not, however, think it wise to put this sentiment into words.

Harry seemed reluctant to let go of Martin's bridle and let him ride into the courtyard. Hesitantly, he asked, 'Just how do you think all this affair of Lord Suffolk will affect us here, sir? The ordinary folk, like me, that is to say?'

'I doubt very much if it will change anything in the slightest,' said Martin. 'A man like Lord Kyme finds it useful to have friends such as Suffolk at court, but it isn't indispensable, as long as he keeps his nose clean, and unless there's some special favour he needs to ask of the King. There'll be no shortage of men looking to take Suffolk's place, or I miss my guess pretty badly, and it would be strange if my lord Kyme had no influence at all with any of them. No, I certainly don't think you have any cause for worry.'

Harry looked relieved. 'You just don't know, do you? Everything seems up in the air at the moment.'

'Natural enough, considering the influence Suffolk has had over the last few years,' said Martin. 'How are the villagers taking the news, or has it not reached them yet?'

'Oh, they've heard, right enough. The only thing that really frightens them is the thought that there might be something in the way of a row between Suffolk's family and friends and the other lot, because in that case they'd be called on to fight for my lord.' He grinned broadly. 'Not that they'd be a lot of use, of course. Hinder rather than help. But that scares them, right enough. Apart from that, any change at the court doesn't really affect us here, you know. A lot of these villagers, especially the older ones, don't even know when their lord dies and his son takes over. Their work, their food and their beds, that's all they know.'

'It saves a good deal of trouble,' said Clement. 'It must be dinner time, surely?'

'Getting on that way,' said Harry. 'I'll give you a hand with your horses, then we'll see if we can't get something to eat, take our minds off this troublesome business.'

Clement had a wonderful knack of moving quickly when there was a meal waiting for him, so the needs of the horses were soon attended to, and they made their way to the great hall. The preparations for dinner were in an advanced stage, but there was no sign of Lord Kyme.

'Probably still preoccupied,' said Harry, remarking on this.

One of the servants came up to them. 'Have you seen Ralph at all, Master Constable?'

'No, not since noon. I expect my lord is keeping him busy. You're waiting for dinner, is that it?'

The man scratched his head. 'Ralph usually lets us know when my lord is pleased to dine. For the matter of that, my lord is not often late for his meals.'

'Well, I'm hungry enough myself,' said Harry. 'I'll try to winkle Ralph out, and see if my lord is of a mind to join us.' He gave a grin. 'If not, then we'll start without him, though it might be as well if we did so in the kitchen.'

'I'll come with you,' said Martin, 'for I want a word with Lord Kyme, if he's not too preoccupied.'

Harry led the way to the wing containing the private rooms, and stopped before the door of what Martin knew to be Ralph's own chamber. The door was closed, and there was no answer from inside when Harry rapped on it.

'As I thought, he'll be busy with my lord.' Harry moved a little way down the passage, and stopped before another closed door, where he hesitated, obviously reluctant to disturb Lord Kyme if he were busy, then tapped gently at the door. There was no answer. Harry knocked again, louder this time, and still there was no answer. He looked at Martin. 'This is odd.'

'Is the door unlocked?' asked Martin.

Harry raised an eyebrow, to indicate that he did not propose to try the door just yet. 'They may be in my lady's room.' He moved a short way down the corridor, stopping before a door which stood ajar. Harry cautiously put his head round the door, then opened it fully, showing that the room was empty.

'This is all very strange,' muttered Harry.

'Have they left Kyme?' asked Martin.

Harry shook his head. 'Can't have done. I've been keeping watch outside since that messenger brought the news of Lord Suffolk, just to be on the safe side. I'd have seen anyone come or go. No, they must be in the house somewhere.'

'Let's take a look in my lord's room,' said Clement.

'I don't really like to,' said Harry.

'We may find a hint as to where they are, though,' said Martin. 'For it's all a bit worrying as it is, isn't it?'

Harry still did not look happy at the suggestion, but returned to Lord Kyme's room, and knocked at the door, louder this time. There was still no answer. Harry turned to Martin. 'Should I take a look, sir?'

'Yes, go on, man. If anyone queries it, I ordered you to go in.'

Harry tried the door. It was not barred from the other side, and swung open. He looked a question at Martin and put his head round the door, then seemed to stagger, and turned back to Martin, his face ashen.

'Well? What is it?'

Harry waved a hand at the door, unable to speak.

'Come on, Clement.' Martin stepped boldly into the room, Clement close behind him, and stopped, horrified.

The body of Lord Kyme lay sprawled over a chair. The top of his skull had been crushed, as if by an axe or club, and his face beaten so as to be almost unrecognizable.

The body of Lady Kyme lay in the centre of the room. She had been killed by a single blow to the head from the same weapon that had been used to kill her husband.

Martin felt a wave of nausea flood over him, but knew it was important to investigate further. He drew a deep breath, and moved further inside the room, alert lest the murderer might still be in there, but it was empty.

Clement moved over to the bodies, checking each in turn. 'Been dead some short time, master. An hour or two, I'd say.'

'You're sure?'

'Aye. I've seen enough corpses in my time to know that much. I wonder why he's so much more battered than her?'

'That's easy enough. My lord put up a struggle, and had to be overcome with several blows. My lady evidently was easier to deal with.'

Martin leaned against the wall, and took several deep breaths. When he felt more in command of himself, he went out into the corridor.

Harry was still looking pale, and Martin took him by the shoulders. 'Pull yourself together, there's much to be done.'

'Aye. Sorry, sir, it was the shock of it. I'll be all right now. But who could possibly have done this?'

'That's what we must discover, and quickly. Now, first of all, what's become of Ralph? Has whoever did this done likewise to him?' Martin went to the door of Ralph's room, knocked, without getting any reply, then, dreading what he might find, pushed the door. It did not move.

'Here, give me a hand.'

Harry put his shoulder to the door, but it did not budge.

'Ralph must be inside, then, for there's no lock on the door. It's barred from the other side. Here, Ralph! Open up! You're safe now,' called Harry.

There was no reply.

'This is a bad business,' said Martin.

'Aye,' said Harry, 'he must have found them, just as we did, and the sight scared him out of his wits. God knows, it almost did the same to me, and I had you two for company.'

'It's not surprising,' said Martin, 'it turned my stomach. Stay, though – perhaps Ralph saw whoever did it, and it was the sight of the deed itself that terrified him.'

'We need to question him, that much is plain,' said Harry. 'I'd best get a couple of men and we'll break the door in, if he won't come out,' and he turned on his heel, making as if to go downstairs.

'One moment.'

'Sir?'

'I think you said you'd seen no-one come in or out all day?'

'Aye, that's so.'

'Then whoever did this dreadful thing must still be in the house, or somewhere about the outbuildings.'

Harry nodded. 'It must be so. I'd not thought of that.' He hesitated. 'But there have been no strangers here, I'll swear to that.'

'Set a guard on the gate,' Martin went on, 'with orders that no-one is to leave unless you give the word, whoever they may be. Clement, you go with Harry, fetch a couple of the men, and we'll try to get Ralph to come out and tell us what he knows, for it does seem as if he's too terrified to know what he's doing just now. Then we'll all of us set to and make a search, see if we can find whoever it might have been.'

The other two nodded, and went off to do as he said. Martin tried Ralph's door again. 'Ralph, won't you come out and talk to me? It's me, Master Byrd. You'll be quite safe, Harry and Clement are fetching help.'

There was only silence by way of a reply. Martin called out again, repeating his remarks in as soothing a tone as he could manage. This time, he was heartened to hear a scraping noise, as if the bar, or whatever had kept the door shut, were being moved.

'That's right, Ralph, you're safe enough now.'

Ralph opened the door, and crept halfway out, like a cautious snail. His face bore a curious look, a look which Martin could not place, beyond thinking that it was not ordinary fear.

'Safe?' Ralph looked around him, and gave Martin a sly little grin. 'Aye, we're all safe enough now, I warrant you. Who safer?'

'Pull yourself together, there's work to be done.' Martin spoke more sharply than he had intended, for he was certain that the horror of what he had just witnessed must have turned Ralph's brain, and it might be as well to use gentleness, as much as possible. 'Now, Ralph, if you should chance to know who had anything to do with this dreadful business, you must tell me. It's your duty, both to Lord Kyme – God rest his soul and that of his poor lady wife – and also your duty to your country's laws, for Sir George and the others will need to look into this as soon as they get here.'

Ralph looked puzzled. 'This dreadful business, say you? No, no, Master Byrd, you're wrong there, quite wrong, I fear. After all, with Suffolk dead and gone, then all those linked to him must needs go as well. Don't you see that, Master Byrd, or is it too subtle for your cleric's wit? Aye, there'll be new men running things now, and therefore the old must be rooted out. Dreadful, indeed! Perfectly sensible, I should have said. Praiseworthy, in fact. For those who engage in the work of cleaning out the old decay and corruption may surely expect some reward, some small preferment, by way of thanks for their efforts?' He looked earnestly at Martin, and added, 'Would you not agree?'

This was all said seriously that for a moment its meaning was quite lost on Martin. Then, knowing full well that the question was both foolish and unnecessary, but quite unable to stop himself, he asked, 'Then you killed them?'

'Aye. There should be some thanks for that from whoever may supplant Suffolk, don't you think?' And Ralph looked anxiously at Martin for approval, for all the world like a little boy who is unsure whether praise or punishment will follow his actions.

Martin was acutely conscious of the fact that he had not the slightest idea what to do next. There was a poor lad back in his home village, who spent all day, every day, summer and winter alike, in the woods, crooning softly to himself, and harming neither man nor beast. Apart from him, Martin had never met anyone whose reason had given way entirely.

Martin turned quickly as he heard a sudden loud clatter of heavy feet on the stairs behind him, and Clement's voice calling out, 'I'll be there in a moment, master.'

That broke the spell. Martin turned back to Ralph, and, keeping his voice as level as he could, said, 'Come now, Ralph. This matter has to be –'

Too late, he saw the heavy iron poker in Ralph's hand, the hand that had thus far been concealed behind the door. Unable to do anything more than hunch his shoulders and lower his head to avoid the blow, Martin could nevertheless plainly see the dried blood on the poker.

Then a searing pain shot through his arm and shoulder, and he crashed to the floor, and for a moment or two was aware only of vague sounds behind him.

Someone shook him violently by the shoulder – the injured shoulder, naturally – and a wave of nausea swept over him.

'Master? Are you hurt?'

'That,' said Martin, 'is the damn-silliest question I've ever heard. And if you must shake me like a terrier with a rat, could you use the undamaged parts of me?'

Clement looked deeply offended, but moved his brawny arm to the other shoulder, and helped Martin to stand up.

With an effort, Martin straightened his back and looked round at his rescuers, Clement, Harry, and a couple of the Kyme men-at-arms, who all stood looking anxiously at him.

'It was Ralph,' he told them.

'What, Ralph did this?' Harry sounded as if he could not believe his ears.

'Aye. And Ralph killed my lord and lady Kyme, into the bargain. Clement, you may be a clumsy oaf – let's face it, you *are* a clumsy oaf –· but I was never more delighted to see anyone in all my life. I truly believe that, had you not appeared when you did, that lunatic would have killed me too.'

'But, Ralph?' asked Harry again.

Martin nodded. 'I know it's hard to believe. I didn't really believe it myself, though he admitted to killing them – nay, he boasted of it, rather – until he hit me.'

'But why?' asked Clement and Harry together.

'I can't say. He had some rambling tale of having to remove all those who favoured Suffolk, of a task to purge the land of corruption – God alone knows what else. It's plain that he's quite mad, my shoulder will testify as to that.' He rubbed his arm, which now ached abominably, but moved readily enough, showing that no bones were broken.

'Better, is it?' asked Clement.

'Better than it was, at any rate.'

'What weapon had he?' asked Harry, wanting to take charge of the situation.

'A big iron poker. There was blood on it, I could see that, so he'd evidently used it to kill the others.'

'And you didn't see where he went at all?'

'Not I, I was swooning with the pain. He can't have gone far, though, for he left as you arrived.'

'I thought I'd seen a movement of some sort at the little door there,' and Clement pointed to the end of the corridor.

Harry nodded. 'Aye. He couldn't go down the main stair, for we were coming up it, so he must go that way. There's a little stair there out to the roof, the battlements.' He gave a smile of grim satisfaction. 'Well, we have him now, for I put a man on the roof to keep watch, things being as they are.'

'But has your man been there all day?' asked Martin.

'Aye.'

'So he cannot know what has happened to Lord and Lady Kyme? He will have no suspicion of Ralph.'

Harry swore. 'That's true.'

'Is there any other way down from the roof?'

'Yes, there's another little stair, the fellow to this one, on the far side. Hey, you,' he told one of the men-at-arms, 'you clear off, watch the other stairs. If Ralph tries to come down, don't waste words, shoot to kill. And you,' to the other soldier, 'give me your bow.' The man handed it over, a short and wicked-looking crossbow. 'Now,' said Harry, setting off towards the little door, 'let's see how the bastard likes fighting a man who can hit back.'

Martin set off after him, but Clement held out an arm. 'Master, you're not fully recovered yet.'

'I'm well enough. We ought to be on hand, as official witnesses of whatever may happen.'

Clement, knowing that there was no use arguing with Martin in certain of his moods, sighed, and put an arm round his master. 'Come on, then.'

The narrow little door led to an equally narrow flight of steep stairs. There was no sign of Harry, and Martin made his way up to a second door at the top, with Clement pushing from behind as best he could. Arrived at the top of the stair, Martin went out on to the roof, and almost bumped into Harry.

'No sign of Ralph,' said Harry, waving a hand.

Martin looked round. There was a narrow path round

the whole roof, with a low wall to one side, and the roof of the house proper to the other.

'What's that?' he asked. 'Looks like a man, stretched out in the angle of the roof, there.'

Harry looked, and moved carefully to the spot Martin had indicated. He bent down, then looked back and waved to them to follow.

'This is my man,' he told them as they reached him. 'The silly sod must've let Ralph creep up on him.'

'Nay,' said Martin, 'he could not have known. Is he dead?'

'No, but he'll have a headache that'll teach him to be more careful,' said Harry, a grin of relief on his face. 'Now, where's the other fellow? Ah, I see him,' and he gestured with a thumb.

A score of paces off, Ralph, with the poker still clutched in his hand, was scrambling over another corner of the battlements.

Harry called out, 'Ralph!'

Ralph stopped, and looked back at them.

'What ails you, man?' Harry called to him. 'Why did you kill my lord and lady in that fashion?'

'Why, don't you see, Harry? With Suffolk gone, the world's changed, and we must needs change with it. The old ways have to go along with the old rulers. New men for a new world. Yes, that's it. Do you really not see?'

Harry looked round at Martin and Clement. 'You both heard that?'

Martin nodded.

Harry moved a pace or two, the crossbow hidden behind his bulky form. 'Come down, good Ralph, and let's talk.'

'Oh, no! I know well enough what you want.' Ralph looked round him, and began to move away.

Harry raised the crossbow, aimed and fired. Ralph stopped, half turned to them with a look of utter disbelief on his face, then slipped and fell, only the battlements preventing his body going over into the moat.

'He should have remembered that I've won many a flitch of bacon for my shooting,' said Harry grimly.

Martin felt a sudden reaction, a great wave of mixed relief and nausea washed over him. Clement, by his side, evidently felt the same, for he let out a great sigh.

'A bad business, this,' said Harry.

'Aye. And it could have been far worse, too,' said Clement, speaking with some difficulty.

'Oh?'

'The whoreson fellow was quite mad, wasn't he? Crazed with envy and jealousy and the good Christ alone knows what else. You said earlier on that I could be in danger, didn't you, Master Byrd? When I think what he might have done to me –' Clement's voice broke, and his body was racked with a great shudder. 'Here, help me down these stairs, will you, somebody, for the love of Heaven?'

Twelve

'A pretty kettle of fish, this,' said Sir George, crossing himself as he looked at the bodies of Lord and Lady Kyme at noon the next morning.

Martin had thought it best that the commissioners should see the bodies for themselves before they were moved to the church, and so had ordered them decently laid out in their own chamber.

After the excitement of the chase, and Ralph's death, there had followed an unsettled evening and – as far as Martin at least was concerned – a sleepless night.

The only slight consolation was that Fortunato had turned up safe and sound around supper time, having been sleeping in a convenient hedgerow, and thus having missed all the excitement. This circumstance had cheered Martin up slightly, for he had half expected to find the dwarf's bloody body somewhere about the house.

And then, Martin, not knowing just when Sir George and the others might arrive, and expecting them at any moment, had not thought it worth sending a messenger in the direction of Norwich. But they had not arrived, and Martin eventually sought his bed towards midnight. Sir George and the others turned up mid-morning, already in a sombre mood, and Martin had mumbled his tale almost before they had dismounted.

'And Ralph's in the stable, you say?'

'Yes, Sir George. It didn't seem right to –'

'No, just so. Well, we'd better view his body, too, make it all official, as it were. You say he confessed to the murders?'

'He did, and in so many words. Clement, Harry and myself can swear to that, if needs be. And there's the testimony of the man he struck on the roof, not to speak of the way he attacked me.'

'That seems final enough, then. Gentlemen, if you are quite ready?'

Once the commissioners had completed their grim task, Sir George called Martin and Clement to a discussion in the great hall. Harry was there as well, as was Fortunato.

'Now,' said Sir George, 'let's take this one step at a time. We'd best tell the local parson, make arrangements for the funerals. Did they have any children? Kyme never mentioned any, and I wonder who his heir might be.'

Harry shook his head. 'They'd no children, sir. Which may be a blessing, come to think of it, for who can say what might not have happened to the poor creatures if they had? As far as I know, the nearest family is up north, near the Scotch borders. The parish priest will know for certain, he's a learned man and drew up a testament or memorandum for my lord as to the disposition of the estate, as I recall.'

'Very well,' said Sir George, 'so it looks as if we can rely on the priest to a great degree. There only remains the question of who's to look after things here until the heirs can take possession.'

Martin coughed. 'If I may, Sir George?'

'By all means.'

'I was wondering if old Master Middleham would

consent to move in as a caretaker? That might even have the effect of ending the old feud, especially if the heirs know nothing of the matter?'

'An excellent notion. What say you, Harry?'

'Well, sir. The old gentleman's well enough liked, for himself, as you might say, but, to speak plainly, he is of the contrary faction to what my lord was, and that may mean that some will not take kindly to him being here, telling us what to do.'

'H'mm. Any bright ideas?'

Timmons said, 'If I may, Sir George. How would it be if I remained, since my family is – or was – heavily involved with Suffolk? I'm in no hurry to return to London anyway, and perhaps the old gentleman might consent to give me the benefit of his knowledge of the neighbourhood when needed. Between the two of us – and the parish priest, if he knows what's what – we should keep things going until the lawful heirs can take over.'

'A good idea. That way there can be no accusations of partiality. You can continue to keep the account books up to date, until the heirs come along, or there's some other instruction from the Lord Chancellor. Anything further?'

None of them could think of anything, so Sir George told Harry to contact the priest, so that the last rites might be properly carried out. 'Though I don't know where Ralph will end up,' he added, 'the local crossroads, I expect. Serve him right too, the treacherous dog. Shame it worked out as it did, but at any rate we can give my lord Kemp a complete statement of the case.'

'Oh?' It was out before Martin could think about it. 'Can't we?'

'What of Master Wood, then?'

214

'Oh, I take it Ralph did that, too,' said Sir George. 'If I'm not mistaken, you had entertained some suspicions of him yourself, Martin, from the very outset.'

Martin nodded. 'That is so, Sir George.'

'Fellow was obviously quite mad,' said Sir George. 'Pity we didn't spot it at once, but there were other possibilities to be considered.'

'Yes, a most puzzling case,' said Killane.

'You can give yourself a pat on the back, Martin, for having suspected that it was Ralph,' said Sir George.

Martin, his shoulder still smarting when he moved his arm quickly, winced at the thought.

'It was a pity that we – and I put myself top of the list,' said Sir George handsomely, 'failed to act quickly enough to prevent this last tragedy.'

'Oh, I don't think anyone could blame us for that,' said Timmons quickly. 'As Mr Justice Killane says, a very difficult case.'

The rest of the day was spent checking the inventory, a prosaic enough procedure, but an essential one if there were not to be any possibility of a dispute with Kyme's heirs later. Clement had disappeared at the start of these necessary but boring activities, and did not turn up until the dinner hour.

'All done, master?'

'Yes, thanks. We missed your valuable help, of course, but we managed – just – in the end.'

Clement looked affronted. 'I thought it might be as well to sound out opinion in the village.'

'And?'

'Oh, as Harry said yesterday, they're never too bothered by all this sort of thing. That is, it's been a shock, naturally, Lord Kyme and his lady being killed in that brutal way, and there was a bit of muttering, but I told them that Master Timmons would be looking after things until the rightful heir came along. It doesn't make that much difference to the labourers exactly who is enjoying the fruits of their labour, you know. Things are just as bad, whoever may occupy the castles and palaces.'

'So there's no likelihood of any unrest hereabouts?'

'I shouldn't think so. And we'll be back home tomorrow, then, master, with our work complete.'

'So it would seem, good Clement.'

Thirteen

They were up early next day, for Sir George wanted as early a start as possible. Breakfast was a communal affair in the great hall, and they were all affected by mixed emotions, with the satisfaction of a task completed somewhat overshadowed by the way things had turned out.

The final preparations were made in an hour or so, and Timmons accompanied Sir George and Killane as they crossed the bridge and set off on the road to the village.

Once again, Clement had disappeared, and Martin waited impatiently in the great hall, now deserted, for all the servants had turned out to see the procession depart. Eventually, Clement arrived, looking as cheerful as ever.

'Where've you been? The others set off five minutes since.'

'I had to say goodbye to – someone.'

'Well hurry up.'

Clement started for the door, but had to step back to allow Fortunato to come in. The dwarf bowed. 'I've come to say my farewells.'

'How will you fare?' asked Clement.

'Oh, Bella and I may serve to amuse Lord Kyme's heirs. If not, then we'll be reduced to tramping the roads, performing for the countryfolk. Not a brilliant way of earning a living, but we'll manage.'

'Are things well between you and Bella?' asked Martin.

'Well enough.' But Fortunato's face told a different story.

'Indeed?'

'She likes me well enough.' It was said in a tone that was almost defensive.

'But you don't like her?'

'Oh, no, I like her considerably. But – well, to speak frankly, I can't – well – you know.'

'What, the old – you know?' asked Clement.

'Aye. That.'

'Why's that, then?' Clement wanted to know. 'Is it because – you know?'

'Oh, no. Not every part is stunted, you know.'

'Then what is it?'

Fortunato shrugged. 'Who can say? The fact remains, though Bella is willing enough, nay, positively eager, when I approach her, I am unable to do a thing.'

'Perhaps it's conscience,' said Martin quietly.

Clement looked puzzled, but Fortunato merely stared at the ground.

'It may help to talk about it,' said Martin.

'What's to say? You evidently know.'

'Know what?' asked Clement.

'Why, that I killed Master Wood.'

'But Ralph killed him!'

'No,' said Martin and Fortunato together.

'Didn't he?'

'No. I did.'

'But why? He brought you up, didn't he? And then he found Bella for you.'

'That's what puzzles me,' said Martin.

'Brought me up?' Fortunato laughed. 'He made me.'

'What d'you mean?'

'What I say, Master Clerk. Do you know nothing of crushed daisy? Of knotgrass? No? Why, there's no reason why you should. But these pleasant little plants, fed to an ordinary baby, will produce the results you see in me.'

'That's witchcraft,' said Clement, crossing himself.

Fortunato shook his head. 'No witchcraft, though there's devilry in it, I'll grant you that much. No, just as willow bark will cure your ague, or dandelion make you wet your bed, so these things, and others, will stunt any child, any normal, ordinary child. I learned that from Master Wood. I learned much from him. You know, I almost looked on him as a father. And I was grateful to him. For Bella, I mean. I never meant to do it, you know.'

'I don't for one moment believe you did,' said Martin.

'Young Robert told the truth. He did lose his knife. I found it, soon after I spoke to him that day. I kept it with me, intending to return it, if not that afternoon, then when I next saw him. Then, later, I saw Master Wood speaking to Daisy, the maid. I knew well enough what he was about, but it didn't bother me. Why would it, when I had Bella? A short while after, I went outside, a call of nature – I fear I'd been drinking rather more than was good for me, and strong celebration ale, at that – and there was Master Wood, coming out of the stables, and sprucing up his clothes. He spoke to me, in the friendliest imaginable fashion, asked about Bella. I don't know what happened – the drink, it must have been – but I saw Bella as she might have been, had it not been for Wood, or someone very much like him, just a merchant, not a wizard, not in league with the devil, but happy enough to use his foul potions for evil. I saw her tall, like Daisy. You've seen Bella, she's lovely. If they hadn't – well. And

I had the knife there, in my hand, and –'

'And then? After?'

Fortunato shrugged. 'Then I went back to the feast. I was sick with the thought of it, but there was nothing to be done.'

'Well,' said Clement. 'As Sir George said, here's a pretty kettle of fish. What's to be done, master?'

'I can't say. Sir George is convinced that Ralph killed all three of them. By rights, I suppose we should tell him.'

'But what good will that do?' Clement wanted to know. 'It won't help Ralph to be guilty of only two murders and not three.'

'It might help me, though,' said Fortunato. 'It's not just this thing with Bella, but I see his face always before me.'

'Do you repent of it?' asked Clement.

'Repent? Aye, if repentance means never being free from the thought of it, I do.'

'Master,' urged Clement, 'you could give him a penance, absolve him. I know you never have, but you could.'

He was right. Martin had taken Holy Orders, he could give absolution, though he had never done so. He sighed. 'I don't know.'

'It would save his soul,' urged Clement.

'Father Gerald is the man to see, though. Why did you not speak to him?' Martin asked.

Fortunato shrugged. 'He was Lord Kyme's man. I don't mean to imply that Father Gerald would violate the secrets told to him in confession, but you have to be realistic.'

'Go on, master. Think of how you'd feel if it was you,' said Clement.

Martin sighed again. 'Very well. Fortunato, you will

climb the steps of the church in the village on your knees, and say three Aves and four Paternosters on each of them.' And then, for the first time in his life, he pronounced the cleansing words that he had heard so often, in the most sonorous and convincing way he could manage.

Fortunato's face lit up. 'A thousand thanks, Master Byrd. If ever you're in these parts again, you'll know where to find one friend.'

'How could you know it was him?' asked Clement, as they walked to the stables.

'Oh, I don't think I did, not until just now, when it all fell into place. I couldn't see who it might be, though, not from the start. Nobody had a reason, you see, not even a most unlikely one. Then there was the knife. It was quite blunt, and yet it was bloody to the hilt, so the blow had been delivered by a strong man. Did you notice Fortunato cracking those nuts the other day? His arms are powerful enough.'

Clement nodded. 'It sometimes happens that a weakness in one part of the body is made up for in another. But –'

'Yes?'

'I'm only an ordinary chap, of course –'

'Well?'

'Well, but does it not seem to you that even a blunt knife might be driven in to the hilt when a big man falls face down on it?'

Martin clicked his tongue in annoyance. 'I never thought of that. But there were other facts that had a bearing on the matter.'

'Of course, master, of course,' said Clement with a grin.

'Well, for one thing, Wood must have known his murderer, for the wound was in front, and Fortunato was the one man – apart from Bertram – who knew him best. And it seemed to me that Wood had been bending down somewhat, for otherwise a heavy blow to the chest would send him over backwards.'

'I see. All quite simple really, when you think about it, isn't it? And what of Fortunato?'

'What of him?'

'His soul, I mean. Do you think he'll be called to account when – later on, I mean?'

'As to that, who can say? I don't think he intended any harm, it was more in the nature of an accident. If he hadn't chanced to find that knife, who knows?'

'Well, let's hope your absolution and penance help him, master.'

'The Church says they will. Who are we to argue?'

'There is just one thing,' said Clement. 'He's such a little chap. Wasn't it a bit hard on him, making him go up all the steps of the church on his knees?'

'Don't you think a penance should hurt, just a little?'

'Perhaps so. But still.'

'If it doesn't hurt, where's the penance?'

'Even so.'

Martin looked at his servant. 'And furthermore, the village church only has three steps. And they're very shallow. As you would have seen, had you visited it.'

Clement stopped, and stared Martin in the eye. 'Master Byrd! What time have I had to go to church, being preoccupied solving this mystery as I have? No doubt, had I had sufficient time at my disposal, I should have been able to mooch about counting the church steps, just like you. And now, shall we go, before the others

get too far ahead? Dinner in London tonight, eh, master?'

Notes

(i) For a review of the way in which the local adminis-
tration of law in England had broken down in the
middle of the fifteenth century, and a note on the
work of the special commissions of oyer and terminer, the interested reader is referred to *Politics
and the Nation, 1450–1660*, by DM Loades. (Fontana,
1986.)

(ii) The use of plant extracts – daisy, knotgrass, walnut
etc – to turn children into dwarfs has been well
documented. (Tesere Taruffi, *Storia Della Teratologia*;
Fortunato Liceto, *De Monstrorum Causis, Natura et
Differentiis*; and see more recently Andrew Allen in
the *Observer*, 18 November 1990.)

Shakespeare was familiar with the practice, as *A
Midsummer Night's Dream* shows – 'Get you gone dwarf/
You minimus, of hindering knotgrass made . . .'

Andrew Allen's fascinating article, the original
inspiration for this book, explains that the plants
concerned produce allelochemicals, which stunt the
growth of nearby plants, thereby reducing competi-
tion, by inhibiting cell division. Allen ends with the
more optimistic information that the allelochemicals
are currently being investigated as a possible cure
for cancer.